Enchanted

Erotic
Bedtime
Stories
for Women

I dedicate this book to you.

NANCY MADORE

Enchanted

Erotic
Bedtime
Stories
for Women

Spice

ENCHANTED: Erotic Bedtime Stories for Women

ISBN-13: 978-0-373-60509-5
ISBN-10:   0-373-60509-9

www.Spice-Books.com

Printed in U.S.A.

Foreword

It is amazing how confused everyone seems to be about women's sexuality, including women. Women's magazines are constantly giving advice about how women can better please their men (and where to find the products to help them do it), while women's TV bombards us with horror stories about how terrible men are—and thrown in the middle of all this we have myriads of dazzling female sex symbols supposedly forging a path for our total sexual empowerment. So why are increasing numbers of women reporting an overwhelming uninterest in sex? Why isn't sex fun for women anymore?

In my opinion, these self-proclaimed representatives of female sexuality in the media are alienating women sexually, by exploiting them, tearing down their self-esteem and raising their expectations of themselves to unattainable highs while lowering their expectations of men to ridiculous lows. When a popular female icon starves herself, alters herself, misrepresents herself, sells herself, exploits herself, etc., she is contributing to the overall standards that influence how women are viewed by men and how they view themselves.

It is my belief that to really empower women sexually (or in any other part of their life, for that matter) we need to stop trying to control or change them. We must accept them exactly as they are. When women feel good about themselves they feel better about sex. Sex is not a market that is cornered by a select few. All women have it within them to be sexual, although it lies dormant in many of us because of the damage done by our culture and media. It can be reawakened, but only through total acceptance of who we are. We need to feel safe being sexual without the fear of being exploited, changed, categorized, punished, shamed or degraded.

I thought erotic stories written especially for and about women might help, and the results of my efforts are the

stories you find here. They are based on the real
fantasies of women, as they are, without censure.
Do not be alarmed if you find a fantasy or two that is
not quite "correct" from every point of view. Bear in
mind that I have carefully selected these fantasies from
the most popular according to my research. Accepting
these fantasies will not harm the movement for women's
equality, since equality can be achieved only through
acceptance.

And so I have accepted and even embraced women's
fantasies and written about them as honestly and fully
as I was able. Keeping in mind that I was writing for
women, I empowered my heroines in ways that would
not compromise the fantasies or the reader. Recognizing
her desire for romance, I added passion and tenderness
to make the sexual fantasies more meaningful. I forbore
the tendency so many writers have to make their heroines
unnaturally beautiful and "perfect." The male characters
carry more than their share of the fantasies, and the
female characters are written so that the reader can easily
imagine herself into the starring role. The stories are highly
erotic, but completely without the profanity and vulgarity
that often accompany sexual material. The characters
are the long-ago friends that most of us grew up with in
Grimm's and other fairy tales. In place of the old, outdated
maxims of the original fairy tales I have slipped in a few
modern adages of my own.

Naturally, it was not possible to include every woman's
fantasy in this book. I chose only the most common and
straightforward for my fairy tales, and I hope that those of
you who are more original and creative than the rest of us
will forgive me for leaving yours out. Every fantasy is not
for everyone, but it is my own personal fantasy that you
find the stories exciting and entertaining.

Thank you for reading *Enchanted: Erotic Bedtime Stories
for Women.*

Beauty
and the Beast

My name is Beauty. It is likely that you have heard of me. My story, or rather, the one they tell of me, has been told too many times to count. But that is not really my story at all. The particulars have been disregarded entirely. I would have thought that with all the telling of it someone would have, just once, stumbled upon the truth. And perhaps some of you did read between those illusory lines and suspect the truth, incredible and shocking as it is. Or maybe the truth is really too fantastic to believe. I admit there are times when I can hardly believe it myself, and it all seems like a faraway dream.

In fact, some of what has been put down in the various accounts of my life is true, for, in order to save my poor father's life, I did consent to live with a fearsome creature that was more beast than man. It is also true that I fell in love with the Beast. As for what happened after that, the storybooks are quite accurate in their exposition for the Beast, immediately upon my avowal of love, was released from an evil curse and returned to his original form as a charming prince. We were married that very day.

But that is where the similarities between the legends you have read and my own incredible narrative end. For I have not lived "happily ever after" since that day.

You see, I miss my Beast.

As I languish here within the lonely halls of this castle, my mind often drifts back to the very first day I spent here. It was with much trepidation that I left my bedchamber that day, very cautiously, to make my way through the vast corridors that twist and turn throughout this fortress. Despite much speculation over the matter (for I had slept not one wink the night before), I could not imagine why the Beast had requested my presence there. I spent the day alone, wandering in and out of rooms and exploring the unfamiliar surroundings, while trying to guess what was in store for me.

This is not to say that I came to the great castle of the Beast against my will, for I was quite anxious to leave the poverty and boredom of my childhood behind me, and so when obligation awarded me this adventure, I was not entirely dissatisfied.

I could not have said what a castle should look like, but it seemed to me that everything I saw was exactly as it should be. Very austere-looking ancestors silently gazed down at me from the lofty positions where their portraits hung superciliously upon the walls. Other walls displayed splendidly woven tapestries of French picnics, Italian vineyards and other exotic affairs. The furniture was intricately carved from the finest lumber, and the carpets were extravagantly thick and colorful. In short, everything was quite extraordinary in its elegance and splendor.

I did not chance to meet the Beast while roaming the castle that day. He had, upon my arrival the previous evening, instructed a servant to take me directly to my bedchamber after I had bidden my father a quick farewell, and watched with strange detachment as he loaded two brimming trunks onto his coach. These were gifts from the Beast, who instructed that they be filled with treasures for my father to take away with him. It calmed and pleased me to imagine my family's delight when opening those trunks.

I did not stir from my bedroom during the remainder of the night, sleepless though I was. I pondered the end of my old life during the long hours of that quiet night, and even into the next day as I drifted from room to room, examining everything at leisure, without seeing a single soul about the place.

Supper was announced with the tinkling of a bell, and it was there that I once again encountered the Beast. Despite his gruesome appearance and gruff voice, I was pleasantly surprised to discover that he was, in fact, a gracious host, and we passed that first dinner with pleasant conversation and food and drink that delighted the palate.

As soon as the meal was concluded, the Beast rose from the table, surveying me with his dark eyes for a moment before asking, "Will you marry me, Beauty?"

I stared at the Beast in utter astonishment. What was I to do? Though my heart was hammering a loud warning of caution not to anger the Beast, I somehow managed to whisper, "No, Beast."

The Beast merely nodded bleakly, saying, "Very well, then," in a tone that indicated he had expected my reply, and he abruptly left the hall.

Relieved that I had not provoked the Beast with my refusal to his preposterous request, I too left the dining room to retire for the evening.

Have I forgotten to describe my bedchamber? Do not think it is because the room was not worth mentioning, for it was, and continues to be, the most beautiful room I would find in this elegant castle.

When first entering the chamber on the previous evening, I was too preoccupied to take much notice of my surroundings. On this night, however, I darted from one thing to the next, examining the wonderful array of objects that had been placed there for my pleasure, until at last my eyes beheld the extraordinary bed upon which I was to sleep. Along its towering posts it displayed, in great detail, the carved images of wild animals, spiraling along the edges and seemingly moving upward until, at the top, there sat a beautiful man with a crown. I knew not the meaning of the exquisite carvings that lanced that wooden frame, but gazed attentively at them nonetheless, for their beauty was not lost on me in spite of my humble upbringing.

Beside the bed an enormous bouquet of no less than one hundred fragrant pink roses stood placidly in an oversize vase that had been set on the bedside table. And, upon my word, from that day forward I was never to enter my chamber of an evening without finding an equally remarkable display of freshly cut flowers beside the bed.

The bedding was every bit as magnificent as everything else I had feasted my eyes on that day, and a shiver of pure delight ran through me as I slipped between the sumptuous silken sheets. It was such a pleasurable feeling that I was momentarily tempted to remove my nightdress. Instead, I ran my hand slowly across the bedding. My senses were rapidly becoming engulfed in exotic sensations amidst the influence of such luxury.

I was startled out of my enchantment suddenly when there came a light rapping on the door of my chamber.

"Who's there?" I inquired, sitting up and clutching the silk sheets about my neck.

"It is only I, your servant, the Beast," came the gentle reply.

His manner was as reassuring and appealing to me as his appearance was frightful. "Do come in," I said, more at ease.

The Beast opened the door to my bedchamber but did not step over the threshold. Through the dim light of the hallway, I could clearly see his physical outline, which would have been terrifying if not for his gentlemanly demeanor. I waited for him to speak.

"I only wished to inquire if all was satisfactory, My Lady," he said, remaining just outside the doorway.

"Satisfactory?" I echoed, suddenly amused. "Good heavens, no! I would never in my wildest imaginings have dared to describe these accommodations as 'satisfactory.'" I smiled happily at my little joke, as I flung the extravagant bedclothes aside, and reached toward the nightstand to light the lantern.

The Beast remained silent and stared at me as if stunned. Upon seeing his expression, I realized my flippant reply must have insulted him and immediately tried to put matters right.

"Oh, Beast! What I meant to say…well, of course every thing is quite satisfactory. Why, it is more than satisfactory! That is what I meant of course."

But something was terribly wrong. It was as if the Beast had not even heard me. Without thinking I leaped from my bed to approach him as I made another effort to explain. But I only managed a few steps before freezing in horror.

Had I heard a growl? My mind reeled between shock and disbelief. It was impossible! And yet, his eyes had a most unnatural glow. He stood perfectly still, like an animal that is poised for an attack.

"Beast?" I whispered, as much a plea as a question.

And then all of a sudden he was gone.

I stood there many moments afterward, trying to collect my shattered wits. I glanced down at my trembling hands, and it was then that I noticed my dressing gown. It was completely sheer, from head to foot! The lantern I had lit only served to emphasize my nakedness beneath the cloth!

I did not see the Beast again until suppertime the following day. There, he was as gentle and refined as I had remembered him being at the previous meal we had shared. I blushed and shivered whenever his eyes met mine, but he never gave any indication that he noticed, or that anything had transpired that warranted such an attitude. His demeanor eventually lulled me out of my suspicions and fears, and I was once again at ease, and even enjoying his conversation and friendly manner. Afterward, he stood up and asked me the same question he had asked on the previous night, and the one he would ask every night thereafter.

"Beauty, will you marry me?"

To which I always replied, "No, Beast."

Our friendship blossomed. And yet, every noise I heard from within my bedchamber at night would leave me anxious and sleepless, waiting breathlessly for that light tap on my chamber door.

But the Beast never ventured near my bedchamber again.

It was I who, unable to sleep one evening, stumbled across the Beast's private chamber while wandering toward the library in search of something to read. I heard a noise, much like a groan, coming from the other side of his door as I passed. I stopped abruptly.

In a moment or two I heard the noise again. I knew immediately it was the Beast and was seized with compassion for him. Was he ill?

Without further thought I knocked on his chamber door. Moments passed and I knocked again.

"Go away," I heard the Beast say at last, in a pleading tone.

"I shall not," I replied determinedly, "not until I have seen that you are well."

Silence again.

"Please," I implored, knocking again. "Just open the door and let me…"

"Go away from that door, Beauty!" the Beast commanded harshly. "Leave now or you will endanger yourself!" His tone was controlled, but his voice was desperate.

I have wondered many times why I did not leave him then. I have told myself that I could not leave a friend in need. I have told myself that it was my curiosity that would not let me leave. I have told myself a great many things, but I suspect that you will not believe them, either.

I turned the doorknob and opened the door to the Beast's private bedchamber.

It was pitch-black inside. I took a few steps into the room, searching the darkness for the Beast. The door behind me suddenly slammed shut. The hair on my neck stood up.

The darkness was slowly giving way to shadows. My eyes scanned the massive room frantically, seeking the Beast's form. Suddenly I heard the shrill screech of metal rings on rods, nearly causing me to jump out of my skin, as one heavy velvet drape was yanked aside so that the bright moonlight could enter the chamber. Now I could see the Beast clearly as he approached me. I could also suddenly hear his irregular breathing, and I realized he was panting.

My own breathing became more rapid as I desperately struggled to get enough air into my lungs. It was as if the huge chamber had shrunk to half its size upon my discovering the

Beast's large form. Fear was steadily trickling through my veins, infusing me with an acute awareness of everything around me. The Beast slowly approached me until he stood so close that I could feel his warm breath on my skin, and I fancied I could even feel heat from his stare. He was a full foot and a half, if not more, taller than I, with shoulders that extended a distance of more than three times the size of mine. There was an unnatural glow in his dark eyes. I shivered in spite of the heat I felt coming off him.

"If you don't want your nightdress to be destroyed, remove it now," the Beast said at last. His tone was matter-of-fact, but his manner was strained, as if he was struggling to maintain control. His voice was gruff, and so deep as to be barely able to transmit human language. His presence engulfed and overwhelmed me. His gaze hypnotized me. His breath burned me. There was nothing that I could perceive remaining of the mild friend I had shared so many suppers with.

And yet, as I stared into the Beast's eyes, mesmerized, a new sensation was rapidly creeping up from deep within me, mingling with the fear.

Utterly motionless, except for my throbbing heart, I contemplated my predicament (meanwhile, as I stood pondering, the foregoing sensation persisted and grew, so that I felt strangely excited and excitable). In this state, I saw the situation only superficially, and reasoned to myself accordingly: What power had I to resist the Beast? Indeed, resistance seemed unlikely while the Beast stood towering ominously over me, silently waiting for me to obey his command. What he was capable of, were I not to comply, I didn't dare speculate. The Beast who stood over me at that moment appeared ready to pounce at my slightest movement. And yet, vaguely,

I suspected the Beast would make every effort to submit to my will, were I to try to escape him.

All the time that I stood there deliberating, which seemed to me like hours, but more likely was mere seconds, I was plagued with that gnawing excitement that had been steadily growing within me, and haven't I as much as admitted already that I was not desperate for the scenario to end?

With a sudden motion, I hastily removed my nightdress, lest my resolution wane. I stood waiting with much agitation for the Beast's next move, but he merely stared at me in silence for what seemed to me an interminable amount of time. I wondered if he could hear my frantic heart; its echo was thundering loudly in my own ears.

The Beast slowly lifted his huge hand and lightly caressed my face. I gasped in shock when I felt it. It was so rough as to almost inflict pain with the slightest touch.

The Beast's eyes flared with momentary anger, but then quieted as he studied me with troubled eyes. "I do not want to hurt you, Beauty," he murmured. "It is you who controls the destiny of us both."

I could not grasp the meaning of his words. His presence was slowly overpowering me, enveloping and entrapping me in its dangerous power. It seemed as if he were warning me of something. Had he said that I was in control? *Should I stop him?* I wondered. Could I still stop him? I felt too weak to move.

Meanwhile his hands, which were quite large as I have said, and clawed, crudely rubbed my tender skin, slowly working their way to my breasts. To my surprise, my nipples immediately responded, hardening under his touch. A moan escaped my lips as he squeezed them; the brute force of his hands combined with my own continually growing desire was agonizing.

He continued to touch me and, when he reached the place between my legs, I felt a wave of shame as my own excitement became evident. The Beast was now changing rapidly; with each passing moment he was becoming more like a beast and less like a man.

"On your knees," he grunted, between heavy breaths. I stared at him, speechless. The reality of what was happening suddenly dawned on me. He would take me just as he would an animal. It was too late to change my mind, however, for he was already brusquely maneuvering my body into the position he commanded right there on the floor. He did this so swiftly and efficiently that I had no doubt left about his strength, or the futility of my trying to escape.

I remained motionless where he placed me for several moments, while the Beast, meanwhile, hastily worked behind me to remove his clothing. Still too frightened to risk angering the Beast by turning to look at him, I could only wonder frantically what lay behind the elaborate garments the Beast took such pains to hide himself in. But my curiosity eventually got the better of my fears and, almost without my willing it to, my head turned in the Beast's direction. An involuntary gasp escaped my lips.

The Beast was unclothed, except for his shirt, which hung open, revealing a torso that was covered in coarse animal hair. From the waist down his body resembled that of a lion's, with two huge paws for feet, and a long tail that hung to the floor. But even more frightening than anything I have described so far was the object that jutted out just below his waistline. It was of a deep reddish purple color and inhuman in size. I was certain that I would never be able to withstand it.

The Beast heard my gasp and caught sight of me staring at

him in horror. He let out a terrible roar that had only the smallest resemblance to the words, "Turn around!"

"You will kill me!" I cried, in real terror, even as I obeyed his harsh command.

"I promise you will live," he replied, with a sudden return to his former gentleness. His voice trembled with his effort to speak. "This is the way it must be until you free us both from this fate."

I was bewildered by his words, but I had no time to dwell on them, for suddenly I felt his breath, hot as steam, between my legs. Even with this warning, I was completely unprepared for what followed.

As rough as sandpaper and larger than the leaf of an oak, the Beast's tongue slowly wriggled and dug itself into my most tender place. I nearly jumped out of my skin, but the Beast held me firm, even as he repeated the action again, and still again. At once aggravated and enthralled by the harsh persistence of the inhuman thing that continued to rub and pry at my delicate flesh, I could do little more than twitch and jerk, one moment desperately trying to get away, and the next moment pressing myself toward him. His large tongue easily covered my exposed area in its entirety with one rough stroke, and then carefully resumed its invasion of my inner flesh with the enthusiasm of a hungry animal. I was near the point of swooning, so overcome with excitement was I.

At last the Beast stopped with a grunt, and I felt his oversized fingers prying me open. By now my entire body was shaking violently.

In spite of my excitement, I felt an immense pressure as the Beast began to press himself into me from behind. I protested with little cries, and my body instinctively edged forward in an effort to escape the intruding Beast. This he would not allow however, and his powerful hands grasped my waist harshly, jerking me all the way back until he entered me. I screamed.

With visible difficulty, the Beast struggled to retain what little human restraint he still possessed. His whole body shook as he held me firmly in place and, in a strangled voice, he insisted, "You will get used to me in a moment."

But I was getting used to him before he finished his statement. My entire body suddenly felt like it was on fire. I moaned, tentatively rocking back and forth. But there was much more than what I had thus far experienced to endure. Pulling my hips forward in short little jerks, the Beast began a steady but gradual advance.

"Slowly," I heard him murmur, possibly to himself, as he continued to edge himself into my body. Little by little he pushed forward, all the while holding me firmly in place. All I could do was remain motionless, gasping and whimpering, one moment in extreme pleasure, the next in exquisite pain.

I would never have thought it possible, but I was, in fact, able to take the Beast entirely. Yet I could scarcely breathe when at first the Beast filled me completely, for I felt as if I were being impaled. I was conscious of nothing but that part of me he filled.

Very slowly, with ragged breathing and low growls, the Beast began to move himself in and out of me. He continued the slow pace for quite some time, allowing me to become completely accustomed to him; but at last his grunts and moans became wilder and louder, and likewise his strokes became rougher and quicker. His breath seared the skin on my back. His hands bored into my flesh, bruising the tender skin. I thought I felt his teeth nip my shoulder.

I was aroused to the point of pain. With my inhibitions long gone, I began to touch myself to enhance the pleasure as I struggled against the Beast.

But I was too late. With a deafening yell and one last hard thrust, the Beast filled me with a tremendous deluge, the excess of which flowed down my trembling legs.

I was profoundly disappointed and attempted to pull myself away from the Beast, but he held me firmly in place, remaining inside me, still fully aroused, as he reached around for my hand and replaced it between my legs. He held it there until I grasped what he wanted me to do.

I was momentarily embarrassed by his knowledge of what I had been doing, but that quickly disappeared as my enthusiasm once more returned. Realizing that I had as much time as I wished to enjoy the Beast, I once again began to stimulate myself. Meanwhile, the Beast slowly pulled himself out of me, almost to the very end, and then, just as slowly, pushed himself all the way back in. He continued this patiently while I sought my own pleasure.

My every sense was awakened and aroused. My skin prickled under the rough hands that grasped my hips. My ears were ringing with the raw, animal sounds that echoed throughout the moonlit chamber. My eyes were riveted to the spot on the floor that displayed the images of our two contrasting shadows as they struggled intimately against each other. My inner thighs were sticky and wet. I thought about the Beast's sharp teeth on my shoulder as I finally found my own satisfaction.

That began my nightly visits to the Beast's private bedchamber. And for me, each night was more pleasurable than the one before, and I no longer felt embarrassed or ashamed. In fact, my Beast was appearing much less beastly to me, and my affection made him appear, at times, even handsome. Even so, when the Beast asked me to marry him each evening, I gently declined.

One day, some months later, I received a message that my father was ill. At supper I showed the message to the Beast. After reading it he looked up at me in horror.

"Please don't go, Beauty," he begged.

"I must!" I cried. "If anything happens to my father before I see him again I shall never forgive you!"

The Beast was silent for a moment.

"Beauty," he said pleadingly, "if you leave this castle, it will mean certain death for me."

"I don't understand," I replied, annoyed suddenly with all the mystery that surrounded him. It had become an unresolved matter between us that so many questions always remained unanswered. Once again I implored him, "Won't you please explain your mysterious words?"

"I cannot," came the usual reply, but his chagrin at his seeming inability to tell me the truth made him a little more indulgent. "I will not stop you from leaving this castle as long as you promise to return to me in one month," he said. "If you stay longer than that I will surely die."

"I promise," I replied with a sigh, knowing I would learn no more from him on the matter.

"I hope you keep your promise, Beauty," he said miserably. Then he rose to leave, but at the doorway he turned to add, "There will be two trunks put out before you leave. Fill them with as many riches from the castle as you like and take them to your family."

That evening I was more eager than usual to go to my Beast, but there was also much to do in preparation for my journey. I rushed to and fro frantically, all the while longing for the moment when I could be near my Beast and bid him a more personal farewell.

When at last I entered his chamber, I was positively quivering with excitement. The Beast was sitting in a chair in a remote corner of the darkened room. Removing my robe, I positioned myself on the edge of the bed in just the way he liked best, as was my habit. Within seconds I was soaking wet and aching for him. That's the way it was for me with the Beast. It was enough just to wait there, trembling and poised on my hands and knees, anticipating what was to come, to bring about that kind of response in me.

I had not even heard him move when suddenly I felt his crude hands caressing my soft skin.

"Turn around," he said suddenly in his gruff whisper.

I paused for a moment, stunned.

"I want to see your face tonight," he said simply.

Intrigued by something new, I quickly obeyed his request, and turned so I was lying down on my back. I silently watched him as he removed his clothes, able for the first time to observe him openly. He appeared so much more fierce and animallike without his clothing. I shuddered with trepidation as I stared at his naked form. Once again, as on that very first night, it occurred to me that, in appearances at least, he really was more beast than man.

But he is a man, I insisted inwardly, refusing to acknowledge any idea that might, if allowed, somehow bring about an end to these nightly pleasures. Yet I closed my eyes as the naked beast approached.

"Open your eyes, Beauty!" he rasped.

I did so and saw his manhood poised before my lips. He took my head in his hands, but I resisted. The Beast refrained from forcing himself into my mouth, but neither did he yield his grasp of my head.

I stared at the object before me. It was shaped differently from that of a normal man's, besides being larger, and was much darker in color. I tentatively put out my tongue, very lightly and cautiously tasting the object that brought me so much pleasure. The Beast shuddered, and suddenly I was seized with a desire to please him. I opened my mouth and caressed him gently with my lips at first, but soon found myself sucking hungrily. He was so large that I could only take a fraction of him, and that with great effort, but he seemed not to mind this; for what I was able to take I took with relish, clutching him with lips and tongue and jaw.

Abruptly the Beast stopped me and removed himself from my mouth. Pushing me down on the bed he spread apart my legs. I stared into his dark eyes as he approached. There was something shining there—something inhuman. I wanted to turn away, but his eyes held mine. A wave of terror trickled through me.

The Beast growled loudly as he entered me. My legs were stretched almost to the point of breaking as I tried to accommodate his immense form. He rasped and grunted as he mercilessly used my tender flesh. His hot breath burned my skin, and I watched with horrified fascination as his sharp teeth carefully nipped at my shoulders and breasts.

But my terror was quickly being joined by that old familiar pleasure that the Beast had kindled within me. They were both working together with the Beast to bring me toward a passion I had never before experienced. I relished the coarse animal hair that covered his body and the fierce, animal sounds that escaped him as he savagely mated me. I squirmed and moaned as his large, rough hands simultaneously bruised my tender skin and sent shivers of delight just beneath its surface. I cried out time and again, helplessly, pleading and dizzy in the utter agony of such exquisite sensations that came from him filling me to overflowing. Wave after wave of pleasure rippled through me as I vaguely heard the Beast's tremendous roar amidst my own screams.

Before I could even catch my breath, morning had come!

I left in such a flurry of activity and excitement that I did not think of my Beast for many days. My father recovered quickly upon my arrival, and I became reabsorbed in the eventful days of a large family. Too quickly my month was up, and it was time for me to return to the castle.

No doubt the stories that you read made me seem quite unkind, and even unwilling to return to my Beast. Nothing could be further from the truth. I missed him terribly! I wanted more than anything to return to the castle, but my dear mother wept each time I made an attempt to leave.

Nearly two months passed in this way, until late one evening I awoke with a start from a dream of the castle and my Beast. In the dream all was dark as I wandered through the halls of the castle in search of my Beast. Upon entering his bedchamber, I found the Beast sleeping peacefully in his bed. As I approached him, it slowly occurred to me that my Beast was not sleeping at all, but dead! It had been my scream that awakened me.

Suddenly I remembered the Beast's warning that he would certainly die if I extended my stay for longer than a month!

I immediately jumped from my bed and packed my things. By morning I was ready to leave and, after a sad but firm goodbye, I began my journey home to the castle and my Beast. Oh, how I suffered that day, worrying that I should never see my Beast again! If only I had known how true that would be…

When at last I arrived at the castle later that day, I immediately rushed to the Beast's bedchamber. The Beast was lying on the bed, exactly as he had been in my dream.

"No!" I screamed, as I rushed to his side. "Please, Beast, don't die!"

His head moved slightly when he heard my voice. I wept with joy and threw my arms around him. "Thank goodness you're not dead," I kept murmuring through my tears.

"You came back," was all he said.

"Yes, I'm back…for good!" And I knew I would never leave him again.

"Will you marry me, Beauty?" he asked.

"Yes, Beast," I said through my tears. "Yes, yes, yes!"

Barely had I uttered those words when, suddenly, there was a great flash of light. In the next instant a strange man sat where the Beast had been lying only a moment before. My Beast had disappeared. I gasped in astonishment and took a step backward.

"Oh, Beauty," exclaimed the stranger. "Finally you have freed me from the curse!"

I blinked through my tears as I tried to comprehend the man's words. He was explaining that he was my Beast, who was really a prince who had been turned into a beast by the spell of an evil witch. Being an especially wicked witch, she had cruelly added the seemingly impossible condition that the prince would be released from the spell only if his true love would agree to marry him while he was still a Beast!

So this stranger is my Beast, I thought, amazed. I examined his face and saw that he was indeed a handsome prince. I could not account for the disappointment I felt and besides, I had never seen my Beast happier than he was on that day. We married.

And now I must end my tale, as it is late and time to prepare for my husband, the prince. He comes to my bedchamber now and, as always, I shall be ready for him when he gets here.

But I shall not search his eyes for that savage glow.
Or listen for that deafening roar.
I stopped looking for those things years ago.

Bluebeard

There once lived a wealthy gentleman who had acquired property throughout several kingdoms. He traveled extensively from one to the next, never staying for any length of time in any one place, so that no one knew just where he resided or what he did and with whom. Because of this, there was much curiosity and speculation about the man.

This circumstance was further aggravated by an irregularity in the man's aspect that seemed to confirm his apparent eccentricity, for he was so unfortunate as to have a beard that was blue. His mysterious lifestyle combined with his peculiar appearance tipped the scales of favor against him just enough that he became, perhaps unjustly, regarded as a man of disreputable character. His surname was abandoned and forgotten, and he was known simply as Bluebeard.

The mysterious life of Bluebeard was a regular topic of conversation among the neighbors of his various mansions, castles and estates, and, with each story that was told of him, his reputation became more and more scandalous. It was, in fact, widely believed that Bluebeard owned his many properties for the sole purpose of housing numerous wives. And when those wives failed to materialize, it was further decided that they must have met with some unfortunate disaster. Who these women were or what exactly it was that happened to them, no one could say for sure. Nevertheless, the ladies shrank back in fear whenever Bluebeard approached.

Now it came to pass that one of Bluebeard's neighbors was a widow who had two grown daughters. Upon visiting his property in that region, Bluebeard noticed the daughters, and shortly thereafter he revealed to the widow his desire to marry one of them, leaving the choice of which to the daughters themselves. But the widow's daughters, upon hearing of Bluebeard's offer, passed him back and forth between them, as neither one could bear the thought of having such a frightful-looking husband with so uncertain a past. In this way they put him off repeatedly until at last Bluebeard, in an effort to win the affection of one or the other, invited them to be his guests in one of his castles far away. This they readily agreed to, as they were curious to know how Bluebeard lived, and to see if the rumors about his exceptional wealth and eccentricities were true.

So it was that the widow and her two daughters, along with a large party of their closest friends, came to stay in Bluebeard's castle. They all remained as his guests for an entire month, which flew by in such a flurry of parties, fine dining and other types of merriment that no one wanted to leave, least of all the widow's two daughters. In fact, the visit went so well that the older of the two sisters began to think that Bluebeard was not quite so fearsome to behold, and even that his beard was not so very blue.

A short time later Bluebeard and the widow's oldest daughter were married. And in spite of the rumors about him, his new bride found Bluebeard to be a loving and attentive husband who spared no expense in giving her everything she desired; she settled happily into her new life with him.

But as everyone who has ever been married knows, there is much one doesn't learn about their spouse until long after the wedding day and well into the marriage. Bluebeard's wife discovered this one day, as her husband prepared to leave for an extended trip that would detain him for no less than a week on a business matter requiring his immediate attention. His wife was disappointed that her husband was going away so soon after their wedding, but Bluebeard kindly suggested that she amuse herself during his absence by throwing parties and filling the castle with guests. He handed her a large ring with many keys attached, giving her access to all of the rooms in his castle and his belongings therein, so that she might have any single thing her heart desired.

But all of a sudden Bluebeard's countenance darkened and, becoming very grim, he pointed to a tiny, odd-looking key that was attached to the ring. Showing this key to his wife, Bluebeard explained that it opened the door to a small room at the end of the corridor on the very bottom floor of the castle. Without offering further explanation, Bluebeard rigorously forbade his wife to use the key and enter the room, warning her that she would suffer greatly if she disobeyed him. Though she made one attempt after another to gain a reason for this injunction, none was forthcoming. Bluebeard's wife stared at the odd little key as her husband bade her a tender farewell.

Now you may think that Bluebeard's wife was eager to send for her friends and throw a great party but, in fact, as she stood at the window and watched her husband's coach ride out of sight, she was overcome with curiosity to know what was in the little room at the end of the corridor on the bottom floor of the castle. Indeed, the poor lady could think of nothing else, so that she was utterly incapable of finding any pleasure in the many luxuries that lay before her.

Clutching the little key to the forbidden room, she wandered up and down the long, winding hallways of Bluebeard's castle, brooding over the warning issued by her husband. At length, she found herself standing at the very doorway of the room she had been banned from entering. "I must have a glimpse inside or I shall have no peace," she reasoned.

Without pondering further over the matter, she carefully fit the tiny key into the keyhole and turned the latch. As soon as the latch was released, the door popped open, but the room was pitch-dark inside, as shutters were closed up tightly over the windows. She rummaged through her pockets in search of a match and, finding one, quickly lit it and held it out before her.

She took a step forward as her eyes, adjusting to the darkness, fell upon a large table. There were shackles attached to the table, evidently for the purpose of restraining someone. Her eyes widened.

In another part of the room she saw a heavy rope hanging from the ceiling. About halfway down on the rope there was a manacle, and directly below that the rope split into two parts, with each connecting to a shackle that was fastened to the floor. On a nearby wall there hung long leather strips of varied lengths and widths.

As she stared at these objects in horror, Bluebeard's wife suddenly recalled the many rumors she had heard about her husband's previous wives, all of which were presumed dead. Suddenly it occurred to her that he must have killed them in this very room, for, to her inexperienced eyes, the objects she saw there could serve no other purpose.

But there was no more time to deliberate over the matter for, at that very moment, the match she was holding burned down to her fingers and with a little shriek, the terrified lady dropped the match and the ring of keys onto the floor. Trembling violently, she felt around in the dark for the keys and, finding them at last, she rushed from the forbidden room, fled down the winding corridor, and slipped into the first open doorway she could find. She collapsed into a nearby chair.

Very slowly the horrified lady began to regain her composure. She assured herself that her husband could not know that she had entered the room—for she had touched nothing. Considering this, she glanced at the key ring and gasped. Was it her imagination, or had the little key to the forbidden room changed? Yes, it had turned bright red!

This discovery started her heart racing anew, and in desperation she took a section of her petticoat and rubbed the key vigorously, but no matter what she did the red would not come off the key. At length she perceived that it was a charmed key, and if her husband discovered it he would indeed find out that she had disobeyed him. But then she reasoned, "If I take the key off the ring perhaps Bluebeard will believe it has been lost."

As she considered this, a dark shadow fell over her and she looked up to find no other than Bluebeard standing before her. She flung the keys behind her and desperately tried to appear happy to see him, but he could see by her face, which was paler than death, that she had entered the forbidden room.

Bluebeard did not accuse his wife immediately, however. Instead, he spoke to her very pleasantly, telling her how, just as he was nearing town, he had come upon a messenger riding in to tell him that the business had been concluded satisfactorily after all, so that he could forfeit his trip. All this he explained in a very leisurely manner, though what it was exactly that he said his poor wife could never have told you, so preoccupied was her traumatized mind.

But at last Bluebeard came to the point and asked his wife very politely for the ring of keys. As you might well imagine, that lady did everything she could think of to delay, but her husband would not be put off, and at length she handed him the keys.

Bluebeard examined the keys carefully and then said to his wife, "Why has the key which I forbade you to use turned red?"

At this his wife burst into tears and confessed all, begging her husband to forgive her. But Bluebeard grabbed her fiercely, dragging her along as he strode purposefully toward the small room at the end of the corridor, saying, "Now you will meet your fate in that room!"

The poor woman beseeched her husband for mercy with tears streaming down her lovely face, so that even the hardest of hearts would have softened, but Bluebeard turned his face away from her and, quickly unlocking the door, forced his struggling wife into the forbidden room just before stepping into it himself. Then he locked the door behind them.

Bluebeard's wife was suddenly silent, as she stood in the dark room and waited. Without the slightest difficulty or fumbling, Bluebeard quickly lit a lantern and set it on a stand near the table with the shackles. Then he approached his wife.

She held her breath in absolute terror as Bluebeard lifted his hand to her face in a gentle caress before placing his hands lower, upon her neck, and carefully reaching under the lace collar of her dress. She shut her eyes tightly, thinking he would strangle her in the next moment. And remarkably, something within her was stirred to life by her husband's touch. She loved him yet!

All at once there was a great tear and her dress came apart, falling away from her in strips. Next went her underclothes and, before her dazed eyes had time to become fully adjusted to the dim light, she found herself standing before her husband without a stitch of clothing on her quivering flesh. She felt fresh tears rushing to her eyes as she remembered how tenderly he had held her only hours before. That he could kill her thus (for that is what she believed he was about to do) left her heartbroken.

Bluebeard led his wife to the rope that she had wondered about only moments before. Very deftly he attached her wrists to the manacle at the center, adjusting it so that her arms were stretched high above her head. Next he fastened her feet to the shackles on the floor, which were set just far enough apart to make it awkward for her to stand. Too horrified to speak, she stood stretched apart, mute and trembling.

Having confined her thus, Bluebeard approached the wall where the various strips of leather hung. As she watched her husband thoughtfully examine them, it suddenly dawned on her what those leather strips were and how her husband would use them on her. With this comprehension came the awareness that her life was not in danger, but she was too alarmed by the unspecified horrors that were still imminent to feel relief over this. She began to struggle against her bindings as she watched him select a thick black whip.

Bluebeard turned back toward his wife, saying, "Because of my great love for you, I shall be merciful. You will receive only thirty lashes."

After a second of shocked silence, Bluebeard's wife began

again, in earnest, to plead for mercy. This he ignored, continuing in the same calm, matter-of-fact tone, only slightly louder to supersede her cries. "You will count the lashes as I give them to you. If you miss a single count, we will start again at the beginning. Also, you must accept the lashes willingly, acknowledging that you deserve them. You may cry out, but you must not protest or I will begin the lashes again."

Immediately after this frightful speech Bluebeard sent the whip flying brutally across his wife's backside for the first time. She cried out, and fresh tears blinded her vision.

"We will begin again," was Bluebeard's cruel reply, and again the lash stung his wife's flesh. This time she called out, "One!"

A moment later another sting from the lash came and she heard herself cry, "Two!" Shock and horror mingled with her shame, and yet, with the next sting of the whip she managed to cry, "Three!"

Bluebeard continued this barrage, and his wife obediently called out the corresponding number to each and every painful sting. Periodically Bluebeard would stop to ask her, "How many more lashes do you wish, my love?" or "Tell me, how many more lashes should I give thee?" to which she was compelled to answer with the full amount due to complete the required thirty lashes. Somehow she managed to do all this, though her skin shone bright red and burned with a white, hot heat, long before her thirty lashes were up.

When at last she had endured all thirty lashes, her husband approached her and gently kissed her face and lips. Although she now knew that her husband was not going to kill her, she still wondered uneasily what more lay in store for her. And yet, she found herself responding to her husband's kisses, partly from relief and partly from a new, curious and incomprehensible need that was growing within her. She began uttering soft words of apology and love. But Bluebeard drew his lips away from hers, chiding her softly, "A loving wife does not take what is not given freely from her husband."

Bluebeard carefully unfastened his wife's hands and feet and, lifting her into his arms, carried her over to the table with the shackles. He placed her gently on the table, adjusting her body so that she was positioned on her hands and knees, with her legs spread wide apart. Her wrists and ankles were quickly and adeptly fastened to the table. Then Bluebeard gently forced her head down onto the table and placed a clasp of sorts around her neck to hold it in place. She was deeply humiliated and agitated to be bound thus, for in this position her most private parts were especially laid open and visible. With horror she realized that her husband had walked to that end of the table and stood before her at that very moment, examining her.

She felt his warm breath on her flesh as he approached nearer, and then something soft and wet touched her exposed area. It took her a moment to realize that it was his tongue, and she moaned with a mixture of pleasure and apprehension. With precision and determination he continued relentlessly, until she was unable to fight off the feelings of arousal that were coming over her. She struggled under the constraints in an effort to enhance her own pleasure. But just before she reached a point of release, her husband stopped, leaving her anxious and fretful. He repeated this process several times, and each time he would test her submissiveness, asking, "Who will you obey from this day forward?" And to each inquiry, what else could she do, besides willingly acknowledge his power and vow to obey him?

Bluebeard continued teasing his wife in this manner for

what seemed to her like an eternity, but suddenly he stopped abruptly and walked to the other end of the table so that he stood directly in front of her. Slowly he unfastened her neck and lifted her head. His pants had been opened, and his arousal stood within inches of her lips.

She hesitated only a moment before she understood what he meant for her to do. Then she took him willingly, eagerly even, for she felt a voracious hunger to please him in any way he would allow. He watched her carefully as she delighted in the pleasure she was giving him.

Urgently she struggled to take him as his thrusts became harder and faster, but when he was about to release himself she drew back, just as he had done with her. At that moment their eyes met, and she saw the silent demand in his. Hypnotized by his powerful gaze, she arched her neck in a submissive gesture, voluntarily taking him, and actually savoring him.

When he was finished, Bluebeard once again placed his wife's head gently upon the table and fastened her neck as before. Then he walked out of the room.

His wife waited in absolute agony for his return.

He returned at last, carrying a small container. Once again he positioned himself at the foot of the table. She waited breathlessly while her husband prepared the next course of discipline for her.

All at once she felt a cold sensation creeping into her body. Frantically she tried to move away from it, but Bluebeard quieted her, holding her firmly with his free hand. Something was piercing her! Something unbearably cold!

She slowly realized that it must be some kind of large object made up of frozen liquid, for she could feel the sharp cold penetrating her, and the subsequent wetness as it slowly melted.

The cold awakened her senses, making them more acute, so that the longing she felt was quickly becoming painful. Yet before the pain yielded into pleasure, the object melted away to nothing. She whimpered as her husband slowly repeated the process, again and yet again, laughing occasionally over her obvious distress. But she was aware of nothing aside from the delightful torture between her legs.

This continued until Bluebeard's wife was feverish and trembling. Seeing her thus, Bluebeard abruptly stopped the agonizing procedure and once again left his wife alone in the room. She moaned softly. There was an excruciating ache pulsating throughout her body that her position made it impossible to recover from. It throbbed painfully at the juncture between her legs, slowly rippling into her torso and limbs. She knew that she would have to wait until her husband chose to relieve her. And she waited.

At last Bluebeard came back into the little room, bringing with him another small container. She held her breath again as her husband resumed his position.

This time it was Bluebeard's hands that she felt, gently caressing her. She moaned in pleasure, but a few seconds later she felt a searing heat where he rubbed, and she cried out in frustration. Bluebeard again quieted her and held her still, but the movement of his hand became more brutal, furiously probing her until she was aware of nothing but the scorching place where he rubbed. But this pain, too, soon gave way to pleasure, and she meandered between screams and moans, one moment shaking her hips furiously in an attempt to escape his tormenting caress and the very next moment working her hips against his hands to enhance the pleasure. But always he stopped when he perceived her pleasure and, scooping up more of the mysterious ointment, he once again began the process, spreading her apart and mercilessly forcing the heat deep inside her.

Finally, the poor lady had endured all she could and she began to weep miserably. Not liking to see his wife so unhappy, and thinking she had been punished enough, Bluebeard quickly unfastened her limbs and lifted her from the table. He held her tightly in his arms and kissed her wet face repeatedly, all the while comforting her with words of love. But she continued to sob.

Perceiving what his wife required, Bluebeard quickly drew her to him and filled her aching body with his own. He made love to her tenderly, and for as long as she wished him to. They remained there, in fact, for the rest of the day, and this time he pleased her over and over again, until all she had suffered earlier was completely forgotten.

As were her promises to obey her husband forgotten, and I daresay they have had occasion to visit the little room again!

Cat and Mouse

The game of cat and mouse is legendary, and is a favorite subject for novelists. What is it that draws one into the game, at once so fascinating and so antagonistic? It is a complicated matter that is ever being examined by the philosopher. I, too, have made many attempts to solve the riddle.

It seems to me that the game was more enjoyable in ancient times. Nowadays it is decidedly less satisfying. Somehow, as the stakes got higher, the players became more menacing and the game more ruthless. In truth, it is no longer even played the way it used to be. For one thing, the object of the game has very nearly been eliminated.

It has long been established, for instance, that Cat is physically stronger than Mouse, but Mouse has nevertheless been a worthy opponent by virtue of her superior instincts and faultless determination. Over the years, however, Cat has accumulated many unfair advantages over Mouse, taking the fair play out of the game. This development has had the peculiar effect of making the game all the more enticing for Mouse, while rendering it tedious and dull for Cat. Such are the circumstances of Cat and Mouse as I begin my tale.

In the story I am telling, supremacy belongs to Cat. Mouse has much less power in most respects: she earns and keeps less wealth, she has a much smaller voice in world events and, in short, she has fewer advantages than Cat. As would be expected under such circumstances, Mouse has lost much of her spirit, and Cat feels the loss without acknowledging it. And so, when he encounters one of those few delightfully tenacious mice who refuse to accept these terms meekly, this new breed of Cat is too frightened to respond appropriately.

Meanwhile, Mouse has lost respect for Cat, thinking him lazy and spoiled by those mice who have acquiesced to his superiority. The game, then, has reached its final stages of existence, and only in the rarest cases, as in the story described here, is it played with the vigor of ancient times.

As my tale begins, Mouse is keeping a low profile in a little hole in the wall in Cat's world. She is dressed in a flimsy rag, which is the modern fashion for the mice in Cat's world, but which barely covers her nakedness and leaves her always feeling exposed and exploited. Still, our Mouse feels relatively safe from Cat because of her rebellious attitude, which his kind interprets as coldhearted spitefulness. This suits Mouse perfectly, for Cat disgusts her.

"Ha! Cowards!" laughs Mouse, as yet another cat scurries past her little hole in the wall, hastening to get away from the hostile creature therein. "How fearful those big, strong cats become when they encounter anger from a powerless little mouse! I shall easily escape the fate of my sisters with mere animosity as my defense."

Indeed, it was not difficult for her to bring forth feelings of animosity. She hated being exploited in this cat-dominated world, never being understood or appreciated for her intelligence and sensitivity. And yet, whenever a cat stopped at the opening of her little den to look her over, she was seized with strange sensations that were both disturbing and frightening. But she refused to let the cats see her fear or, more especially, her secretly harbored hope that she might someday meet a *real* cat, like those she had read about in romantic novels. So she hissed and cursed at them, laughing to herself as they nearly tripped over their own feet in their hurry to escape her.

She set her face in an expression of haughty disdain as she heard another cat approach. He was much larger than she was, as were all the others, but she reminded herself that size wasn't everything. She was certain that her will was superior to his.

She struggled to remain composed as the cat stood in the entranceway, his eyes moving leisurely over her body. The usual agitation burned in her. By what right did cats think they could ogle mice in that rude way? How did it get to the point where this was considered normal behavior? If she behaved like other mice, she was now expected to be flattered to have been honored with his attention! She jerked her chin up even higher and met Cat's eyes with a look of disgust.

He was uncommonly handsome, she grudgingly noticed. It was indeed unusual these days for a cat to care about his appearance at all. They were generally so scraggly and unkempt that it offended one to be anywhere near them. But then, the mice were so busy worrying about their own appearances that it rarely occurred to them to notice that the cats were not worth all the trouble.

This cat, however, was one of the few who would be considered worth the trouble. But that was all the more reason to avoid him in Mouse's opinion, for the good-looking cats were worse than the slovenly ones. They were in great demand and they knew it, and it was hard work indeed to win their affection for a single moment, let alone to achieve any kind of long-term devotion. As she looked at this cat's self-assured expression, Mouse realized he probably had a number of mice at his beck and call. She forced herself to look past his physical beauty.

But it was impossible not to note the thick hair that fell in short dark waves around his face, or the faultlessly chiseled features that arranged themselves into an expression of absolute confidence and poise. His muscular body moved with singular grace and ease. Mouse's sharp instincts warned her that she had better get rid of him quickly. She drew her most effective weapon in ridding herself of cats: her tongue.

"Look all you like, pig," she snarled. "You will never be allowed to touch." For at the very least, this strange world in which she lived would not permit a cat to force a mouse to submit against her will. Indeed, there was not the slightest temptation for them to do so anyway, since mice were offering themselves up willingly to be the eager slaves of the undeserving louts!

To Mouse's astonishment, Cat actually smiled at her remark and then slowly reached his hand into her little hideaway. Very carefully, so as not to touch her skin, he took one agile finger and lifted the ragged material of her covering up to her shoulders, exposing her body completely to his view. With an angry hiss she slapped his hand away.

"You did say I could look all I liked, did you not?" He laughed.

Now, Mouse had one weakness, and it was that she was highly competitive—especially in matters of wit and will.

Hers was a character that was easily drawn into the game of cat and mouse. The cat's clever retort, combined with his easy demeanor and absolute disregard of her bad-tempered manner was sufficient enticement for her to ignore her apprehensions and change her mind about her earlier resolution to get rid of him immediately. It might be better to torment him a bit first.

Her eyes held his with sudden interest, and one corner of her lips turned up in a smirk. She shrugged her shoulders and tried to assume a look of casual indifference. "I was only thinking of you just now," she rejoined with mock sincerity. "I would hate your ego to suffer the singular blow of being refused what you desire."

"It's sweet of you to be concerned for my welfare," he replied with a grin. His eyes burned into hers as he added, "But on that matter we both know you don't need to worry."

She wondered if his remark meant that he did not find her desirable, or if he was just so confident that she would acquiesce to him if he did. He saw her confusion and laughed.

More curious than ever now, she took the coy approach, saying, "I suppose you have too many mice to choose from to become overly excited about any single one, what with the harem of slaves you must have lined up to do your bidding." She said this as if she was complimenting him, but the message was clear enough. One of the things she detested most about this modern cat's world was the way mice were always so willing to debase themselves by selling their flesh to the cats as willing sex slaves. And yet, she knew it had to sting the cats' pride to know that, even though they could buy virtually anything they wanted from the mice, they were, nevertheless, obliged to pay for it. In her remark, she was insinuating that he, too, would have to pay for favors, even though she suspected that it probably wasn't true in his particular case.

Cat was not put off by her remark in the least, however, and with a cool and steady composure he answered, "Even so, I am willing to give you the opportunity of being my slave if you ask me nicely." He loved the way her eyes flashed in anger at his remark. He was enjoying goading her immensely.

"I most certainly do not want to be your slave!" she huffed. How could he twist everything around so completely? She wished with all her heart she could wipe that Cheshire Cat smile off of his face!

"If you didn't secretly wish to be my slave you would not have brought it up to begin with," he argued.

His arrogance aggravated her, and her eyes flashed as her smirk became a sneer. "Could you really be so conceited that you think what I meant by my remark was that I wanted to be your slave?"

"I would bet my tail on it."

"As confident as that, are you?" she challenged, looking for an opportunity to make him see how wrong he was. She was too inexperienced in the game to realize that he was baiting her.

"Shall I prove it to you?" he asked, returning her challenge.

"*Prove—!*" His audacity was really too much. An alarm of some kind flashed a warning inside her brain, advising her to be cautious but she was too provoked to heed it. Besides, it was exhilarating to finally meet a cat with a little bit of backbone and such a quick wit. Ancestral courage welled up within her in response to his challenging posture. She felt it was her duty to put him in his place, and so without another thought she blurted, "If you can prove anything but my utter disgust for you, I will be your slave for this very evening!"

As soon as the words were out she felt a flash of terror. Had she really just said that? And when had she stepped out of the protective shelter of her mouse hole?

It didn't matter. She would never give in to him, and he would eventually be forced to leave her with his tail between his legs, unsuccessful and humiliated. This thought made her smile.

Cat was smiling, too, thinking, just when it seemed that all the mice were docile little fools, ready to submit to anything put before them, he finds this little gem. Why, she was exactly what he had been searching for his entire life. And to think that he had nearly avoided her, at the advice of the many other cats who had rejected her. "Bitchy," they all called her! What fools! As exquisite as she was, it was to be expected that she would instinctively want a cat that was willing to put up a fight for her. He recognized this because he came from that same species of animal as she, who prefer a struggle before mating. He needed to continually prove his right to possess his partner, while she needed a mate that was worthy of her and unafraid. Through instinct he knew that they both felt these things, though he also knew that she did not fully understand them yet.

Cat stepped closer to Mouse and lightly brushed her hair to one side. She felt his warm breath on her face as he murmured, "How shall we put it to the test?"

She sucked in her breath and held it. A thought or two crossed her mind but she remained silent. She was utterly stumped.

"Perhaps a kiss," he suggested finally, after allowing her thoughts to wander a bit.

She sighed in relief. All she had to do was withstand one kiss without swooning over him. She was certain that she could do that. How sweet it was going to be to send him packing after he did his damnedest to impress her with his best kiss. She nearly chuckled at the thought.

He looked in her eyes and saw the amusement there. So she was already congratulating herself on her victory, was she? Good. He needed to catch her off guard. But he warned himself to be careful. She was one-of-a-kind in their world, and he was not about to let her get away.

Confident now, Mouse tilted her head back in anticipation of Cat's kiss, all the while looking expectantly into his eyes. He stared back at her while his lips hovered directly above hers for what seemed like an eternity. An uncertainty came into her eyes, and suddenly she was impatient. Was he going to do it or not? What kind of a simpleton says he's going to kiss you and then doesn't do it?

His lips remained so close that they were almost brushing hers. "Well," he finally whispered, "where would you like it?"

"What?" she whispered back.

"The kiss," he explained. "Where would you like me to do it?"

She stared at him in shock. Images that made her dizzy entered her brain, but she instantly forced them out of her consciousness. And yet she was trembling. She once again reminded herself that the wisest course would be to get this over with quickly.

And just how was she supposed to answer his question without sounding like she *wanted* him to kiss her? He really had an infuriating way of setting her up. What she would really like to do is— Suddenly she had an idea.

"I think the least-offensive place would be my foot," she said at last, with an eager smile.

"Your foot it is," he replied without disappointment. He had expected no less of her. Besides, his suggestive question had had the desired effect. He had noticed her loss of composure, if only for a few moments.

He went down on one knee before her in a deceivingly submissive gesture. As she prepared for her attack, Mouse felt a peculiar disappointment that he had allowed himself to be beaten so easily, and a strange regret that it would all soon be over. It occurred to her that, from somewhere within herself, she had hoped he would be smarter or stronger or something…but immediately she reproached herself for being so foolish, remembering that it was her pride and her freedom that were on the line here.

Cat gently picked up her foot and placed his warm mouth on it for a lingering kiss. Immediately after the kiss was concluded, Mouse yanked back her foot in a swift motion, with the intention of kicking Cat in the face—an act that would once and for all show him her utter self-possession and lack of response to him. But as she swung her foot forward to deliver the blow, his hand flew out with razor-sharp precision and caught her ankle, holding it in a grip of steel. She gasped at this unexpected turn of events. The strength she felt in the grasp he maintained on her leg sent a thrill through her. She tried to shake him off but he held her with as little trouble as she might have had holding a butterfly by the wing. All at once she was completely disarmed.

Suddenly she lost her footing, balancing and struggling on the one foot as she had been. With arms and legs akimbo, she fell, bottom first to the floor. With the swiftness of a panther, Cat reached out and caught her, breaking her fall with his hands. She was at first relieved and then horrified. His hands cupped her buttocks. She moved to get up, but he held her.

"We haven't determined the effect of the kiss yet," he said with smile.

"What do you mean?" she asked, still struggling to get up and away from his hands.

"What I mean," he explained calmly, "is that I want to see if I was able to inspire 'anything but your utter disgust' for me with my kiss."

"Oh…well I can assure you that disgust pretty much sums up my feelings," she lied, trying to appear calm and unaffected. But it was difficult with his strong hands holding her the way they were.

"I don't believe you," he replied. "And I like to verify things whenever possible."

"Well, it's not possible," she snapped back. "So you're just going to have to take my word for it."

"But it is possible," he argued. "It's not only possible, but it's also simple and painless." So saying, he removed his hands from beneath her and pried open her legs.

At last she realized what he meant to do. A persistent tingling had been building up between her legs since before the kiss and now her desire was all but throbbing within her. "No," she protested. "No." She shook her head back and forth as she struggled desperately to close her legs.

"If it's as you say," he said in an annoyingly reasonable tone, loosening his hold on her legs for the moment, "after one brief inspection I will leave here and never bother you again. But if you're lying, as I suspect, you are rightfully my slave for the evening."

She gasped in horror. When did the tables turn and he become the victor?

"You can admit your desire for me directly if you'd rather," he said patiently.

"Never!" she nearly shrieked.

"Well then, you have nothing to hide, have you?" he asked.

His eyes locked with hers, and it was as if she were hypnotized as she allowed him to open her legs wide. His fingers gently touched her, probing her. She cursed her treacherous body even as she shuddered with pleasure when his finger slid easily into the telltale wetness. He let out a hoarse groan and drew her into his arms.

"I win," he said, just before his lips claimed hers.

Her pride was crushed but she could no longer deny that he had won the battle. Still, she conceded grudgingly. Her eyes flashed with anger and she bit his tongue when he pushed it into her mouth. This did not disappoint him in the least; it was again what he had expected from her. He willingly permitted her to vent all her rage on him. After all, he understood how annoying it could be to lose.

He gently held her arms down until she ceased her clawing, all the while continuing to kiss her tenderly. She struggled to fight off her feelings of attraction to such a worthy opponent; but gradually she began to submit to the warm feelings he kindled in her, and finally she accepted her defeat and returned his kisses with a passion that matched his own. She wrapped her arms around his neck and her legs around his body. But he only reveled in her total surrender for a moment. He had already decided that he wanted much more from her than one night of forced servitude. It was time to raise the stakes in their game.

Cat pulled himself away from Mouse's embrace and asked her, "How is it that I, your master, am here servicing you, my slave?"

She was too stunned by the rude interruption to respond. She had thought that her utter surrender to him would satisfy his need to dominate her, but it seemed that she had been mistaken in that. He wasn't waiting for a response from her, however. With a quick motion he slapped her buttocks, saying, "Up, slave."

With burning cheeks Mouse abruptly stood up, attempting to straighten the disheveled cloth she wore, useless though it was. She glared at Cat, silently vowing to find a way to get even with him. But he went on as if he hadn't a care in the world.

"Follow me, slave," he said, leading the way. But before she had taken her first step he added, "On your knees."

She gaped at him, nearly choking on her words with the horror she felt. "I will not," she finally managed.

"You, what?" he asked, feigning shock at the outburst. But it was again what he had expected. He knew it would take heaven and earth to get her on her knees. And as luck would have it, he just so happened to have the power of heaven and earth over her at that particular moment, for he knew her pride would never allow her to renege on a bet.

"You heard me," she remarked, standing rigidly before him.

"Are you, then," he said slowly and evenly, "refusing to make good on our deal?"

She paused at that. "I will serve as your slave for the evening, but not on my hands and knees."

"You agreed to be my slave, and a slave is obliged to do *everything* as indicated by her master," he reasoned shrewdly. "Furthermore, I can assure you that it is quite usual for a slave to be required to take that position…and many others."

At this Mouse was silent. She had never been a slave before.

"Tell me," he continued, "if I were your slave, would I not be on my hands and knees at this very moment?"

Mouse again remained silent, because she could hardly

deny that she would give much to see him on his hands and knees at that moment. Cat felt it was the perfect time to set Mouse up for another game.

"You were the one who proposed the stakes," he reminded her. "Now unless you wish to demand a rematch to win back your freedom, you are bound to serve me however I wish."

It only took a second for her eyes to flash back to life and for her to grasp the hook he had dangled before her. "A rematch?"

"Yes," he said smoothly. Then, pretending to change his mind, he added, "I mean, no. I don't think I could be enticed to agree to that. After all, I've got a pretty good deal here with you as my slave for the evening."

He almost smiled as she uttered the words he had been waiting for. "But we could go double or nothing!"

"Why should I wager two potential nights of slavery for the one definite night I already have?" he asked. "No, forget it. You're wasting time. On your knees, if you please."

"What do you want, then?" she demanded.

"Well, to consider giving up my evening as your master, I would need the opportunity to win something of even greater value to me, say…you as my wife." He was as shocked as she was when he said it, for he had only been intending to make her stay with him for an indefinite period of time. But once the words were out he knew he meant them. He loved the feeling he got from her challenging nature. They had the perfect chemistry, and he knew they would keep challenging each other for the rest of their lives.

But when Mouse heard his words she almost laughed. "You expect me to wager one night of slavery against an eternity of it?" she asked, incredulous.

"As my wife, you would hardly be a slave," he rejoined. "But it is flattering to know that your first instinct is to assume that you would be the loser."

This irritated her pride, and she grumbled resentfully, "It was only by using trickery that you won the last bet. It was completely unfair, and I can assure you that it will not happen again." Although she could not help remembering his prying hand, and wondered how she could make true her rash statement.

"Am I to understand that you wish to undergo the test again?" he asked with a taunting smile.

"No!" she blurted, mortified. She tried to hide her blushing cheeks by turning her head away from him in an arrogant gesture. "What I mean is that I dispute the accuracy of such a barbarian test."

"Oh, I can assure you that it is a more accurate way to find out the truth than by your words," he argued. "What I felt there was definitely not 'disgust.'"

She was annoyed and embarrassed by the reminder. "If you had the impact on me that you suppose, it seems that you could somehow have extracted the truth from my lips."

"Is that another challenge?" he asked.

"I…well," she stammered, a little more wary this time. But all at once she seemed to make up her mind. "Yes!"

He held out his hand to her. "So, you accept the terms—namely this night of slavery against becoming my wife?"

"Those terms are not fair, and you know it!" she protested.

"Whether it's fair or not, I cannot say," he replied. "But it is for me, as the reigning victor, to set the terms, and there they are. Take 'em or leave 'em."

Her jaw was set in an obstinate expression as the anger flashed in her eyes. She would be damned if she would agree to his outrageous terms. "Let's get this night over with," she snapped.

He sighed, silently debating over how long it would take him to break her down to the point where she would accept his terms. He was torn between two and three minutes. He placed his hand on the small of her back and pushed forward gently. "On all fours then, slave," he reminded her.

She took a deep breath, assuring herself that she could do this. But her first attempt failed. Her limbs felt unusually stiff. It was as if they possessed a will of their own, and refused to bend under the present circumstances. Her face was scarlet when she was finally able to force her body to submit, and at length she found herself prostrate before the arrogant cat, on hands and knees.

The position was new to her. She was overcome with shame and mortification. But there was something else. She felt agitated and inexplicably high-strung. Unwelcome tears filled her eyes. She struggled to stifle her sobs so that her tormentor would not know the extent of her discomfiture. He, meanwhile, positioned himself behind her. Though she pressed her legs together as much as possible, she knew that in this position she could not hide herself from his view. The strange stirrings this provoked within her caused the tears to flow faster. She was in a dangerously emotional and excitable state.

Cat's hand caressed her exposed area possessively. He chuckled as he once again felt her wet desire. She gasped, on the verge of panic. *I must regain my composure,* she thought. But there was such turmoil within her that she hardly knew where to begin.

Her captor slapped her buttocks lightly, saying, "Forward, slave." Awkwardly she crawled forward, hating him more with every advance. He walked behind her, enjoying the view, but not really liking to see her so subjugated. He felt that she was definitely at her most magnificent when she stood in a posture of authority.

Tears threatened to gush forth again, but Mouse blinked them back as best she could, determined to maintain an appearance, at least, of internal composure. But with every movement she felt more debased and was quickly giving way to despair.

"Left here, if you please," Cat instructed cheerfully.

She abruptly stopped.

"But that leads outdoors into the public," she protested in horror. By some miracle they had avoided seeing anyone in their travels so far, but she knew that the likelihood of seeing other cats and mice would increase tremendously if they left their current shelter. Surely this fiend who was to be her master for the evening would not be so depraved as to force her to accompany him out there!

"I know where it leads," he was saying. "I have a desire for some fresh air, and you shall accompany me."

"But there are cats out there!" She would not—could not—possibly go out there, where everyone would see her in this position and henceforward think of her as a slave. What was she to do?

He saw the look of wild desperation on her face, but he could not let up now—not when he had come so far with her. He was determined to have her submit to him fully, and he knew that the only way to accomplish that was to win completely. He was amazed that she had lasted this long. But he knew she could hold out no longer. She would rather do anything than to serve him publicly on her hands and knees. And he certainly had no intention of allowing the other cats to see her so demeaned.

With an air of impatience he gently nudged her forward with his leg. "Onward, slave!" he demanded.

She didn't budge. Tears were running down her face. He fought the urge to stop the game and take her in his arms. But there would be plenty of time for that later, and he forced himself to give her another nudge. "Let's go, wench." But his voice was losing its authority. He was astounded by her stubbornness. *Take the challenge,* he mentally implored her; *you will still lose, but at least you'll do so with a little more dignity.*

"I'll take the challenge," she choked between sobs.

He let out a sigh. "Stand up, then," he said, feigning indifference. "Unless you've grown to like it down there."

Mouse shot up like a rocket. She was trembling with relief and busied herself with dusting off her hands and knees as she tried to regain her composure. It occurred to her that she had put herself through all that humiliation for no good reason. What did she care that the wager was unreasonably high? She would not—could not—lose to him a second time, for this time it would require a confession from her lips, and she still had full command of that organ, if not the other parts of her body. No, he could never make her utter in words the same admission her body had given.

Cat led Mouse to his quarters, which, of course, were far superior to her little hole in the wall. It irked her that the cats always had so much more than the mice, especially since the reality was that mice worked just as hard, if not harder than the cats. She looked at him, agitated and uncertain.

"So all I have to do is remain here with you without—" she paused "—without…"

"Without confessing your true feelings for me?" he suggested with a grin.

"Without confirming your illusions regarding my feelings

for you," she corrected, becoming more hopeful and composed now. "And for how long do you plan to keep me here?"

"Will two hours, do you think, be sufficient?" he asked sweetly. "It will by no means take me the full two hours to have you issuing forth a confession of your desire for me, but still, I find two hours to be the amount of time I most prefer to spend in this particular pastime." He walked casually toward the window to hide his countenance from her. He could only defeat her if she took the bait.

"I don't care a fig about your personal preferences," she stormed, wishing that she could just once make him lose his smug self-assurance.

"Is that your way of asking for three hours instead of two?" he taunted.

"Two hours is more than enough time to have to endure your presence," she replied. "And you will be the only one 'issuing forth confessions' of any kind."

He congratulated himself on his ability to lure her in, yet again. She would indeed be a dangerous opponent if she were not so hotheaded. He removed the smile from his lips and turned to face her. "Another challenge?"

"Well…" she thought for a moment. "I do think I could tolerate you as *my* slave for the evening. Yes!"

"Just so we understand each other," he quickly moved in for the kill. "If you declare your obvious desire for me first, you become my wife? If I declare my desire first, I become your slave?"

She thought for a moment. "Yes, I think that sums it up."

"Well then," he said with a smile. "Just so you know, if you're going to have a fighting chance of getting any kind of declaration from me, you're going to have to do it from over there." He flicked his thumb in the direction of the oversize bed that stood in the middle of the room.

Mouse bit her lip as she looked toward the bed. She had been thinking the very same thing. And why not? She would not mind sampling pleasures from the cat who had managed to get the best of her up to this point.

Cat almost groaned out loud as he read her thoughts from the expression on her face. Perhaps he should have taken what he could have from her as his slave. But no, that would never satisfy him. He wanted this mouse forever as his playmate and rival.

He stepped nearer to her and lifted her chin. His eyes locked with hers. Determined to win her heart he lowered his lips to hers. Determined to win the game she met his lips with fervor. Now she could at last give in to the desire that had been growing within her throughout their little game. She wound her arms around his neck and pressed her body up against his. As long as she didn't speak, everything would be all right.

In one easy sweep, Cat lifted her in his arms and carried her to the bed. He wanted to remove his clothes and feel her softness against his skin, but needed the advantage of remaining clothed for as long as possible. He also wanted her to be completely relaxed and at ease, so he prudently dimmed the light. He leaned over her on the bed and very adeptly removed the little ragged cloth she wore. Then he resumed kissing her, while his hands aggressively explored her naked flesh.

Although his hands and lips were sending thrills throughout her body, somewhere in a far back corner of her consciousness Mouse could hear a repeated warning, but it was too distant to make out at first. As she struggled to regain control of her mind, it slowly occurred to her that she should not be passively allowing him to seduce her like this. *She* should be seducing *him*. After all, she didn't just want to avoid losing the bet; she wanted to win. She wanted to see him on his hands and knees, groveling before her, just as she had been forced to do before him.

She raised herself up and pushed her hands against his chest in an effort to force him onto his back on the bed. When he complied, she slowly began to remove his clothes. His body was so beautiful in its masculinity that she could not help but wonder if by undressing him she was not harming her own cause more than his.

Taking a deep breath, she slowly lowered her lips to his face. He tried to claim her lips with his, but she backed away, and then repeated the action, until he allowed her full control of the kiss. Once this tiny battle was won, she began placing her kisses lower, working her way past his chin and neck to his chest, and then even lower still until she heard his sharp intake of breath. She realized then that she had one clear advantage over him, and that was that his desire was visible. She could easily perceive the effect she was having on him. Her confidence soared as she lowered her lips over the distended protrusion that betrayed him. He made one pitiful attempt to stop her before she closed her lips around him, gently sucking on the tip. A low groan escaped his lips. She wondered for a moment if that counted. Surely that groan, translated into language, would be an expression of his obvious desire for her. But she knew she needed more. Well, there was more than one way to skin a cat! She took him farther into her mouth, suffering his size as he came up against the back of her throat. Suddenly he pushed her head away from him.

"What's the matter?" she said, wide-eyed with feigned innocence. But thinking ridicule to be a better tool, she allowed her lips to slip into a wicked smile. "Afraid?" she taunted.

"Not at all," he replied in a forced tone of civility, but a muscle in his jaw was jerking violently. "I simply want more."

With that he jerked her body toward him so that she landed beside him but facing the opposite end of the bed. She knew what he was thinking and started to protest, but he raised his eyebrow with the same challenging look she had given him. And what could she do?

She was not so confident this time, as she once again took him into her mouth. His strong hands curved around her buttocks so that he could hold her body in place as his lips and tongue descended upon her. His tongue, with the accuracy of a compass, landed directly upon the magic spot with its first touchdown. He began a firm circling motion just above and around it. She struggled to move away from her skilled adversary, but he held her firmly in place with his hands as he continued to torment her with his tongue.

She realized suddenly that she had paused in her own attack while trying to defend herself from his. She struggled desperately to gather her senses and concentrate on what had to be done. She grasped him with her lips, licking and sucking him furiously in an attempt to match the pleasure he was showering on her. He was taken aback by her vigorous assault, and his tongue paused as he tried to regain control, but only for a moment. They both shuddered and moaned from the pleasure they suffered at the hands of the other.

But neither would allow the other to be satisfied, for that would render them powerless. Instead, they repeatedly brought each other to the very precipice of release and then stopped short, hoping that the other one would make the plea that would end their torment. Cat was so aroused that Mouse could taste his pleasure, which had been seeping out in small salty drops, the excess from that which had been building up within him and was now bursting to get out. Cat, too, when pulling away from Mouse's tiny, aching membrane, would pause to submerse his tongue in her wetness, reveling in the effect he was having on her. She was so close, he knew. If he could hold out a little longer, he could enjoy these pleasures with her forever. But he realized he had to do something quick if he was going to win. He could feel himself losing control.

Stopping abruptly to change his course of action, he raised himself up over her and spread her legs wide. Her cry, when he thrust himself into her, delighted him nearly to the point of surrendering to her then and there and confessing his desire to have her. He knew it was extremely dangerous, to take her this way when he himself was so excited, but it was his only chance. He was still physically stronger than her, even if she was his sexual equal. With that in mind he bit his lip and took the upper hand in the contest, forcing her excitement to grow. He placed his hand on the spot he had previously held with his tongue and rubbed gently as he drove himself relentlessly into her.

Mouse was so close. Her face was flushed, and she was panting for air. Every muscle in Cat's body strained as he struggled to maintain control, and all the while he watched her every motion with rigor. "Come on, sweetheart," he coaxed.

The moment had come. He saw the vulnerability in her face as she approached her weakest point, and he hated himself for doing it, even as he abruptly stopped the motions that she now wanted more than ever and pulled himself all the way out of her.

She stared at him in shock. Her hand reached down to touch the place that burned to be touched, but he intercepted it and held it firmly down so she could not use it. She struggled under him for a moment.

"Please!" she whispered.

"Please, what?" he asked.

His lips were so close to hers that they brushed her as he spoke. The pleasure was excruciating. Anger flashed in her eyes as she turned her face away from his warm lips and once again struggled beneath him. He slid himself back into her all the way and held himself perfectly still there. Sweat trickled down his back, and every nerve ending in his body was screaming for him to give in to her, to end this torment, but he held his ground. There were tears in her eyes.

"Tell me you want it," he said in a voice that was misleadingly gentle and kind. "That's all you have to do." She struggled again. He didn't want to lose her now.

With slow, gentle thrusts, he began again. His hand resumed its gentle caressing.

"Oh, no," she whimpered.

He smiled in spite of his agony. "Oh, yes," he replied.

Like a well-tuned musical instrument, her body responded in perfect time to his every touch. She was feverish in her struggle, and he was getting impatient. Why did she have to be so stubborn? He was going to make her a very happy wife. When his excitement began to overtake him and he came too close to the edge, he thought about losing her forever, and that was sufficient to cool his desire and hold his own needs at bay.

"That's it," he coached lovingly as she once again came perilously near the brink. "Now tell me that you want me." He pulled himself almost completely out of her again and paused.

"No!" she screamed. But she was referring to his stopping, completely unaware now of what he wanted. "Please…oh, please. Don't stop."

He didn't want to mince words at a time like this, but he couldn't have disputes over the matter later. "Tell me that you want me," he repeated.

"I…" she stopped herself. He pulled himself completely out of her.

"I…" she repeated.

He groaned loudly, thinking she had nearly as much endurance as he had. He pushed himself back into her and held perfectly still.

"Tell me, sweetheart," he pleaded.

"I…want you," she whispered, tears streaming down her cheeks.

Cat wanted to comfort Mouse, but that would have to wait until later. They both had held out for way too long. He thrust himself into her again and again, thinking only to seal his victory with his final satisfaction, but suddenly he recalled the prize he had won and what it had cost her.

Using the very last grain of self-control that he possessed, he slowed his thrusts and once again busied himself with pleasing her. He could not believe, after all that, he had almost forgotten her and gotten himself off without satisfying her. Happy wife indeed!

Cat gathered his wits and held back, concentrating on giving Mouse what she needed. Soon she was again reaching the true object of her struggles. This time he brought her through to the very end, and then with a loud yell he poured himself into her with absolute relief.

They clung to each other afterward, both trembling from the experience. After a while Cat lifted himself up from her embrace to examine her face.

As Mouse regained her composure, a small blush crept over her features. But she struggled to maintain an indifferent demeanor as she boldly met Cat's eyes and said, very nonchalantly, "I must say you caught me off guard that time.…What do you say to a rematch?"

Cinderella

Once upon a time there came to be a fairy-tale princess who wasn't living happily ever after. She was called Cinderella, and it happened that a number of years after marrying the prince she began to wonder if she hadn't been happier *before* her meddling fairy godmother sent her to that ill-fated ball.

For one thing, the once-beloved glass slippers had of late become dreadfully uncomfortable. Cinderella's feet had suffered from the rigid confines of the glass, and she could scarcely endure the pain it caused her to venture from one room to the next, let alone to go outside the castle. Any desire to roam or explore was quickly squelched by the horror of the piercing pain she would have to endure to get there.

The prince had also become a source of displeasure to Cinderella, who felt as confined in her husband's castle as her poor feet felt in the glass slippers. Oh, at first it had been terribly exciting to think that he had chosen her from among all the women of his kingdom to be his wife! When he whisked her away to become his wife, she felt that she really must love him, if for no other reason than that.

But the excitement all too quickly died, and then Cinderella was left with less pleasant sensations. The attentions that her husband bestowed upon her had seemed flattering in the beginning, but in retrospect they appeared to have very little to do with her. His desires and appetites were shocking in their frequency and strength, which ran hot until satisfied, only to dissolve too quickly into nothingness. She at once admired and resented his determination to have fulfillment of those desires. Her initial instinct and aspiration to satisfy her husband had eventually come to feel more like a task. And no sooner was the task complete than he would remove himself from her, both physically and emotionally. In the end she was left feeling isolated and even sometimes a little misused. Yet if these duties were not petitioned at all, she felt even worse, inadequate.

Besides these problems that existed when Cinderella and the prince were together, there arose equally disconcerting ones when they were apart. Cinderella, in her tedium, could not help but wonder where her husband went and what he did when he was away from her. Left out and alone, with only the crippling glass slippers for companions, she felt quite forsaken. She began to envy the prince and the things he did, and even the people he did them with.

It was all so disappointing. And Cinderella was as disappointed in herself as in everything else, for hadn't she done everything in her power to win this position as the prince's wife? Why had she and all those other young women been so actively competing for a man they hardly knew?

Worst of all was the feeling of helplessness. Cinderella was completely bewildered about what she could do to improve her situation. She still cared for the prince, she supposed, but he was not making her happy.

One day it all became too much for Cinderella to bear, and in a fit of anxiety she threw open the doors of the castle and rushed outside. The sun was shining encouragement and the birds were singing a carefree tune that made everything seem possible, so, taking heart, Cinderella began to run. But her discomfort quickly overcame all else and forced her to stop her running and sit down on a nearby log. She began to weep miserably.

Suddenly there came all around Cinderella a soft, tinkling sound accompanied by little, sparkling lights. She looked up with a sense of recollection and, lo and behold, there before her was the fairy godmother of her childhood.

"What ails you so, Cinderella?" asked the kind lady.

"Oh, Fairy Godmother!" exclaimed she. "I am not living happily ever after!"

Her fairy godmother was shocked. It was not customary for her to be called back by the tears of a godchild whom she had already enchanted with her powers. In fact, it had not happened to her before. She sat close to Cinderella and tenderly took both her hands up in hers, determined to find the cause of all this. Could it be that an evil witch had cast a spell on her goddaughter?

"Tell me, dear, what it is that is making you so unhappy?"

Cinderella thought for a moment. How could she explain it? It wasn't precisely that anything was making her unhappy. It was more that nothing was making her happy. Then she remembered the glass slippers. Certainly they were one source of unhappiness that she could clearly identify.

"The glass slippers that you gave me are making me very unhappy, Godmother," she whimpered.

Her fairy godmother drew in a sharp breath. "Why, my dear," she cried defensively, "I was certain they were a perfect fit!" How dare the girl question her abilities?

"Well yes, but they are so *confining!*" replied Cinderella.

Her fairy godmother was stunned into silence by that. What could she say? Who presumed that a glass slipper, or a prince's kingdom, or any other fairy-tale aspiration for that matter, would *not* be confining?

"It's as if I can't be myself in those shoes," continued Cinderella. "I can't even remember who myself is."

"Ah," said the wise fairy godmother. She could not comprehend the connection this complaint had to do with the lovely glass slippers, but as it happened she was very well acquainted with the ever-prevalent issue of self-identity. What fairy godmother wasn't these days, what with frogs who believed they were princes and wolves impersonating grandmothers? And as luck would have it, the recommended cure came in the form of two lovely slippers, the uppers of which were made from the softest part of lambs' ears, and bound together with the wispy tendons of bat wings, and all of this was soled with the rubbery tips of a thousand tiny leaping frogs' fingers. In addition to heightening the wearer's self-awareness and desires, the slippers were above all comfortable, so with a little good fortune they would cure Cinderella of everything that ailed her.

"I do have the cure," her godmother announced, "but I must give you this warning—self-discovery is a solitary activity, and the discoverer must have a care not to alienate those who matter most to them."

Cinderella nodded her head impatiently. Her fairy godmother's warning was too ambiguous to concern her overmuch, especially since she was so discontented as to try anything new, regardless of consequences.

So without further ado, her godmother waved her magic wand and lightly tapped Cinderella's feet, each in turn. They both watched with fascination as the glass slippers magically dissolved away into nothingness. Almost immediately the glass was replaced with the softest imaginable material of the palest possible pink. The exotic material weaved itself elaborately around Cinderella's feet, starting at the tips of her toes, continuing along the arch of her foot, and finally winding itself over her heel and around her ankle. Cinderella's eyes widened in amazement as the remarkable slipper took shape in a most clever design around her foot. She arched her ankle and twisted it this way and that in admiration as she watched, never having seen anything so utterly exquisite before in her life.

Now Cinderella's feet had become all but deadened from the dreaded glass slippers, but very stealthily sensation was returning to them, as a tingling awareness of the magnificently soft material encroached upon all of her foot's nerve endings. She wiggled her toes in approval, and the luscious feeling of her skin moving within the supple slippers sent shivers of delight all the way up her legs. She gasped and squealed with glee. Feeling as if she had the abilities and grace of a gazelle, she pushed herself up onto her toes and laughed merrily as she spread her arms wide for a pirouette. Her fairy godmother smiled as she watched Cinderella. Perhaps she would fashion herself a pair, too…

Later that evening, when the prince returned to his castle, he called out for Cinderella again and again, only to find, again and again, that she was not there to answer him. He was extremely concerned by this, as it had virtually never happened before, and more to the point, there were dangers always present and lurking in their kingdom. There were ogres and witches and even worse in nearby forests, lying in wait for any opportunity to infiltrate their kingdom and cause their mischief. As he searched the castle with no sign of his wife, he grew more and more concerned. Could some mishap have befallen Cinderella?

When he was certain that Cinderella was nowhere within the castle, the prince gallantly mounted his horse and rode out to find her. He circled the castle, and after that the kingdom, in increasingly larger segments, that he might cover every inch through to their borders. As he did this, he stopped at every sign of habitation to ask if anyone had seen Cinderella.

The search continued for many hours until the prince reached a certain tavern from which lively music poured forth. Frustrated and exhausted from his utter lack of success thus far, he thought the tavern an unlikely lead indeed, but unwilling to leave a single stone unturned he wearily slid himself from his horse and went inside.

The prince gasped in astonishment just as the tavern doors were closing behind him. There, directly opposite his gaping eyes, was Cinderella, laughing and dancing as if she had not a care in the world. Her expression was happier than he had seen it in several years, and his outrage was temporarily distinguished by memories of the last time she looked just that way, a long time ago, on the dance floor where they first met. It had been that look that had stolen his heart, blinding him to everything but finding her again and making her his wife.

But too soon after they married, that look had disappeared from her face, and frowns and pouts had taken its place.

Until now, that is.

And much as the prince had longed to see that look on Cinderella's face once again, this was certainly not the setting he had imagined seeing it in. Why was she here? Who was she with? How could she have come here without the slightest regard for his feelings, or even a simple note to advise him of where she would be, which at least would have saved him the efforts of the last agonizing hours he'd spent trying to find her? He was shocked and confused by her astonishing behavior. But his confusion was quickly giving way to anger as he edged through the crowd toward his wife.

At last Cinderella noticed the prince, just as he was approaching, and her face froze for a mere second in stunned surprise before she rushed into his arms. She was breathless and smiling again as she kissed him and whispered happily, "There you are, my darling!"

The prince was completely disarmed by this greeting.

"I was just wishing you were here, and here you are!" she continued, winding one arm around his neck and placing the other inside his warm hand for a dance, which he found himself engaged in even before he willed it. She examined his face with a queer little smile on her lips. She seemed to be searching for something.

With effort he shook himself out of her spell long enough to ask, "Where have you been?" This seemed rather dull-witted, though, since she had obviously been here in this strange tavern, so he added, "Why didn't you tell me where you were going?"

"Until just a few minutes ago I had forgotten all about you" was her forthright reply, spoken so guilelessly that it was impossible to detect offense.

The prince was stunned yet again; becoming, in turns, confused, shocked, annoyed and angry.

"I'm taking you home," he announced, leading Cinderella out of the tavern and lifting her onto his horse. She went with him willingly enough, and without a word. As they rode toward the castle she wiggled closer to him repeatedly, and her arms tightened lovingly around his chest. She felt excited and alive to be riding thus with her husband at night, and it aroused her further to rub herself against the prince while straddling the horse. She felt as if every minute was hers to be enjoyed, lived and spent. She could not bear to let a single moment pass without experiencing some little joy.

The prince was trying to stay aloof but it was nearly impossible for him to remain so while Cinderella was rubbing up against him in such an enticing fashion. He felt that she must be mocking him, but even so he found himself stopping the horse suddenly and pulling her down from it. And then he was once again on familiar ground, tearing at his wife's skirts, knowing what he wanted and that she would willingly comply.

All at once Cinderella jerked herself away from the prince and ran, half-naked, into the darkness. The prince could not see her clearly, but he could hear her fluttering about, laughing childishly.

Cinderella spun around and around in the fields. She could not say why, but she was loath to be subdued and taken just yet.

After a shocked moment the prince followed Cinderella, calling her name out sharply. This amused her all the more, and she laughed the harder as she weaved this way and that in the darkness. The air was cool on her flesh and it began to tingle.

The prince had reached the limits of his endurance by now, and he called out for her once again in the same tone a fed-up parent uses with a naughty child. But Cinderella paid no heed to this, merely continuing her butterflylike weaving this way and that around the prince and his horse.

The prince decided the only way to put a stop to Cinderella and her bizarre behavior was to catch her, which he promptly attempted to do, as he slowly and lithely made his way into the darkness, crouching down low and listening for her laughter and breathing and her light steps as she ran. His body, in anticipation, hardened and tensed. His heart slammed in his chest. He too felt suddenly very alive.

As soon as she perceived that the prince was stalking her, Cinderella ceased her laughing at once. Her breath stopped in her throat. Where was the prince exactly? It was very dark and there were too many shadows to discern which was what. Childish fear played at her fancy but a strange titillation and anticipation was stealthily building up and overpowering the fear.

A few yards to one side of her, Cinderella could make out the darker shadows of a forest. Thinking to hide in these woods, she warily took one step in the direction of the shadows. She stood very still for a moment and listened. Knowing that her husband was somewhere out there in the darkness, listening, waiting, *preying* on her, sent a sharp thrill right through her. She resisted the urge to bolt for the woods and very cautiously took another step. Again she listened but there was no sound. She lifted her foot to take yet another step toward the woods.

But quicker than a wild beast, the prince had her, snatching her by the arm and pulling her to him, so that Cinderella came up against him quite abruptly

. Before she even comprehended her situation enough to scream, he was crushing her lips with his. Her whole body shuddered against his, and feeling her tremble, he lifted his mouth from hers to search her face. In his eyes there was no more anger, only desire. Her eyes reflected that desire, so he kissed her again, but with much more gentleness this time.

The prince moved slowly this time, first carefully laying out a place for Cinderella, then removing her clothes and finally, removing his own. He tentatively put his hands on her, at first simply touching her skin, and spreading out his fingers so she could become accustomed to his warm hands on her cool flesh. His hands roamed deliberately over her body, coddling and loving her first, then becoming more demanding as he rediscovered the places that brought him the most pleasure. He leaned over Cinderella and kissed the tips of her breasts as his hands moved over her belly and down between her legs. She arched her hips and moaned. But the prince's hand suddenly became brusque and even offensive as he rubbed her brutally.

Something in the back of Cinderella's mind recoiled and then came alive. No; she would not let this opportunity pass away from her! She boldly took hold of her husband's hand and stopped his thoughtless chafing. After a brief moment, having got his attention, she placed his hand correctly between her legs, pressing the tips of his fingers into that one particular place that she had always wished he would touch. She moved his fingers very slowly over her flesh in the way it felt best, and with just the right amount of pressure. She sensed his initial shock, but hadn't he, too, shocked her on many such occasions?

The prince allowed Cinderella to lead his hand, trying his best to halt his tendency to grab and plunge, and realized suddenly that he had only been making cursory efforts to touch her there in an attempt to get himself into her, and take her, like some rutting bull.

As one hypnotized, the prince was fully under Cinderella's spell and eagerly waited for her to enlighten him further on her pleasure. It took effort and self-control to hold back and gently and carefully touch the place where her hand was pressing his into her soft flesh, but he concentrated all his energies on what she was trying to show him. She loosened her hold as he became more skillful, and it thrilled him when she moved her hips against his capable hand.

Using the most sensitive parts of his fingertips, the prince very gently felt all around her exposed flesh, searching very vigilantly for a clue to her secrets. Just above her soft opening he discovered a small bud of flesh that appeared to be quite tender. He noticed how Cinderella quivered when he rubbed the little bud in just the right way, just at the top where it begins, in a circular motion, and at just the right tension and speed. It thrilled him to see her tremble and shake beneath his fingertips, and he could not resist every now and then slipping a finger into her, and shuddering when he felt the soft, silky wetness that was the reward for his efforts.

Every now and then the prince, in his impatience, would unconsciously quicken the motions of his fingers, in his impatience to bring about Cinderella's climax, but each time he did this, she would bring him back to attention with a gentle motion of her hand, as a reminder of how she liked it. Each of these little incidents caused another surge of excitement to fill his loins, until he thought he might explode. Even so, he was determined that she should be thoroughly satisfied and would have joyfully administered this pleasure to her throughout the night if she had wished it.

However, Cinderella was presently breathing very quickly, in short little gasps. She had momentarily lost all awareness of the prince, for strange little fragments of sensual scenarios were playing themselves out inside her brain. The prince, meanwhile, could sense that he was very close to bringing his wife the satisfaction she had so often given him, so he focused all his concentration to what his fingers were doing. He forced himself to keep a slow, even pace, as his fingertips relentlessly rubbed and twirled her swollen flesh. Suddenly he realized she had arrived at the peak of her excitement, and it took all his self-control to keep the steady pace until she was fully relieved, but he did just that. And even when she was finished, he very leisurely and gently held her there, and then kissed and licked her there, relishing in her wet silkiness. Cinderella moaned and shuddered in utter contentment.

But by this time the prince's endurance had reached its limit so he pulled himself up and pushed all of his hardness into Cinderella, and it felt better than it ever had before. Her opening had never been so soft and plump as it was after being pleasured, and he held her firmly against him as he moved inside her and tried desperately to hold on to the pleasure for as long as he could. He didn't want it to ever end but he couldn't stop it, either, as he rounded the corner into that exquisite release that passes almost as quickly as it comes.

Afterward the prince held Cinderella for longer than he ever had before, trembling and groaning as he crushed her to him. It was she who stirred first and then he grudgingly moved away from her and began to dress. They dressed in silence, for she was quite sleepy by now, and he held her protectively in front of him for the remainder of the ride home. At the castle he lifted her down from his horse, carried her into their bed, and slipped off her soft little slippers. Then he crept into the bed next to her and they both drifted happily off to sleep.

The following morning Cinderella woke up alone as usual (for she was not an early riser) but beside her she noticed a rose. This brought a smile to her lips but that suddenly froze as she recalled with astonishment the events of the night before. She wondered what her husband made of her strange behavior. She could recall no disapproving remarks from the prince but, then again, there hadn't been much conversation. She remembered her misuse and teasing of him and wondered that it had resulted in such kind and tender ministrations from him.

Cinderella continued to ponder the matter as she rose up from their bed, when there on the floor she spied the little pink slippers. She reached down and picked up one of the little shoes and a strange thrill ran up along her arm. She examined the delicate slipper. It was so pretty and soft that she could not stop herself from slipping it onto her foot, and all at once, she forgot everything but that strong desire to sample all that life had to offer. And once again she forgot about the castle and her husband, the prince.

This day Cinderella felt a keen interest in her kingdom, and more particularly, the people who lived there. She had been so secluded in her life so far, and wished to see how others lived. She wandered about among the towns and shops, seeking knowledge about the goings-on in her world, and where she fit into them. There were so many intriguing things to occupy one and here she had been, holed up in the castle like some Rapunzel, too uncomfortable and afraid to take part in it all. She discovered that there were many pursuits that appealed to her, and the day flew by so quickly that she scarcely realized it had become night.

Meanwhile, the prince had once again arrived home to find that Cinderella was not there. Supposing that she had returned to the tavern, he rode out to meet her there. But she was not at the tavern and no one there had seen her or knew her whereabouts. Once again the prince found himself annoyed with his wife. Though he had been ultimately delighted by her behavior of the night before, he felt in retrospect it had been a bit shocking the way she had wantonly given in to her desires and appetites, only to disappear again this following night. He wondered where she was and who she was with, and envious resentment came over him. Could she have forgotten about him yet again? He sighed with frustration. It left him feeling somewhat inadequate, that she could so easily forget him and enjoy the company of others after he had spent so much effort to please her!

All of these ruminations only served to fuel his anger all the more. He felt suddenly weary and decided to go home and have done with her childish games.

But upon returning to the castle he discovered Cinderella had arrived, and in a jolly mood, smiling and laughing, and not even noticing his sour mood. She chattered excitedly about her day and the many interesting things she'd seen. All seemed harmless enough, and in spite of himself, the prince's mood improved; for it is impossible for any husband to remain angry when his wife is so happy.

Yet the prince felt a lingering anxiety and restlessness. It was as if everything was changing. Would it be for the better, or worse?

He reached out for his beaming wife and drew her to him. She wrapped her arms around him and kissed him heartily. She could feel his hardness as he reached beneath her blouse, but she abruptly drew away from him, offended by his hastiness. Why, it was as if her husband needed only to turn on a switch.

"I feel like a bath," she purred. "Won't you prepare it for me?"

How could he refuse? Sullenly he went to draw her bath. As he watched the water fill the tub he reflected that bubbles might make the bath more pleasant for them both, since he planned to linger while she bathed and he loved the way the bubbles bounced and clung to her luscious curves. This he accomplished easily enough, but then it occurred to him that candles would undoubtedly make the bubbles sparkle as they bounced. These thoughts chased away his surly mood, and he was even smiling when she came in for her bath. She glanced at the candles and then at his face, and she blushed as he gave her a wink. Could he be flirting with her? Her heart gave a little leap.

And even when Cinderella slipped off the enchanted slippers she was still too delighted by her husband's attentions to remember to be unhappy.

Needing a task to take his mind off his throbbing loins, the prince picked up the soap and began to wash Cinderella, starting with her feet, taking time to massage her flesh from toe to heel, slowly and caressingly, and then moving his way up her leg to her thigh. She closed her eyes and moaned with pleasure. He did not rush over the task, but perceiving her wish to relax and unwind from her unusually busy day, and also wishing to enjoy the task ahead of him, her husband leisurely and thoroughly bathed her.

As the prince lovingly assisted Cinderella with her bath, he asked her questions about her day and listened attentively to her answers. The warm water and his courtly manner caused her cheeks to turn pink with warm anticipation. It suddenly occurred to her that her husband was infinitely more attentive and charming and romantic when his body desired her than he was once she had already pleased him.

And his attentions were in turn making her desire him.

The prince had very scrupulously washed her legs and feet, and now his hands very gently and carefully washed her private area. She had been chatting happily until then, when suddenly his administrations silenced her. Their eyes locked as his hands slowly washed the fleshy parts of her opening, and then wiggled into the cleft of her backside and circled that opening as well, not quitting until both regions were squeaky clean. Next he washed her torso and breasts, and shoulders and back. Then he pulled the plug to let the water drain, while at the very same time pouring very warm water over her to rinse her.

The bath was so well performed that Cinderella's heart was touched along with the rest of her senses. For this was not the bath of an impatient lover, but more like that of a loving caregiver. His gentle attentions caused her heart to fill.

Cinderella rose up from her bath and stood perfectly still as the prince took up a large towel to dry her body. She watched his face as he carefully toweled her curves and angles, paying special attention to the crevice between her legs, with extra gentleness, but a meticulousness that left her breathless. He then lowered his attentions to her legs and feet, kneeling before her and taking each foot onto his leg to dry each toe in turn.

The prince suddenly dropped the towel and began to caress Cinderella with his fingers. Still on his knees, he stroked her skin, which was especially soft and rosy and sensitive from her bath. Ever so tenderly he embraced her, kissing her stomach while his hands roamed over her backside in a firm but loving embrace. Cinderella shivered.

Holding Cinderella's bottom in his hands, the prince turned his face to kiss her abdomen, again and again, and then lower, he kissed the cleft between her legs, his tongue darting out in search of the secret little pleasure spot he had discovered the night before.

The prince firmly licked up from the center to the front of Cinderella's open legs; again and again, and as he licked her he wiggled his tongue into her smallest crevices, and twirled it in and around her sensitive nubs and peaks. All his energies were centered on that part of her he explored, so that it seemed his senses existed through his tongue alone, and it was thus that he could see, feel, smell, taste and hear Cinderella.

At last the prince found what he was looking for and he carefully began his relentless pursuit of Cinderella's ultimate pleasure. He whirled and stroked the magical little membrane with his tongue, slowly and meticulously. Her hands instinctively went to his head and her fingers entwined themselves within his dark locks. He felt her shudders as he worked on her, and his ego soared with triumph. Every now and then he could not resist dipping his tongue into her open body to taste her delicious contentment. This would cause both to moan with pleasure.

But suddenly Cinderella desired her husband to join her in this pleasure. In her mind she had conjured an image and she wanted to experience it with her other faculties. So she took the prince by the hand and led him to their bed. Without a word she removed his clothing, leisurely enjoying his hard muscular form as she did, and then finally pushing him gently down on the bed. His body was hard and straining as he willingly complied with her will. She positioned herself beside him in an arrangement that left him no doubt what she intended. She rolled to one side and bent one leg enough to open herself to him, even as she took his entire hardness into her mouth. He clutched her buttocks in his hands and pulled her into his face, as his tongue easily found her tender pleasure spot and resumed its stroking.

Cinderella had never enjoyed having the prince in her mouth quite so much. It had been tiresome, in the past, working over him, trying to please without knowing if she should go faster or slower, or when it was enough. Now she simply relished the feel of him in her mouth, and didn't worry about how she performed, because she suddenly realized that it was all so much easier for *him* to enjoy. So she simply let herself get pleasure from him now, caressing him with her tongue and lips as she marveled at his male hardness. It made her feel exceedingly erotic, to simply suckle and leave it to him to move in and out of her mouth as he pleased. It sent thrills through her when his thrusts forced her mouth to open wider, or when she felt him pressing into her throat. And all the while he never stopped working her with his tongue, so she quite thoroughly lost herself in the sensations of having her mouth and throat opened wide and filled by him, while he kept feeding upon her private parts.

Further and further Cinderella sank into herself, even as she experienced the most intimate joining she had ever shared with her husband. She simply lost consciousness of anything unrelated to her own sensual pleasure.

Lips and tongues were for licking and sucking. Legs were for opening wide, so eager eyes could look inside. Skin was for touching; every part, every cell seemed to be screaming with a mounting pressure to reach that tingling release. This was, at that moment, what she was living for.

It rushed toward her and enveloped her. Then in the next instant it was gone again. And yet there was a milder pleasure that lingered.

This was undoubtedly what her husband had experienced so many times before; and to think she had resented him for it! She had thought she was simply pleasing him, but no! She had been searching for something for herself all along, and now that she found it she understood perfectly why her husband had so enjoyed it.

She lay very still, languidly reveling in the delicious sensations that continued to course through her body. Her husband had not reached his own moment yet, but she knew he would and felt no rush to bring him there. Instead, she savored the blissful responsiveness she felt to him.

The prince moved very slowly to embrace his wife, kissing her face and neck and lips. Her body was languid as he opened her legs and rested between them. She lifted her arms to him, and he entered her body as he embraced her in a deep kiss. He marveled at how incredibly soft and wet and pliable she was. He could not recall ever feeling this aroused. His whole body shook, and she felt like a part of him, she was so wholly his. His release was more intense and powerful than he had ever experienced before, actually bringing stars before his eyes.

The prince did not move for many moments, simply holding Cinderella in his arms while remaining inside her. His mind replayed the events of the night, in great detail, as if trying to unravel a mystery. A strange light came into his eyes.

Why had he never thought of appealing to her senses and enticing her body to open to him, instead of merely taking her? How could he have so arrogantly disregarded the secrets to bringing her body pleasure? His own pleasure was increased tenfold with this subtler kind of taking; not to mention that his manhood soared when he witnessed the absolute power he could wield over her mind and heart and body—not the power to *have* those parts of her, but the power to excite and thrill and titillate. He swore to himself that he would never again miss this important and exceedingly pleasant part of their joining.

And finally Cinderella really did live happily ever after!

East of the Sun
and West of the Moon

There once lived a man who was so poor that he could barely feed his family. They lived in a rundown cottage in a remote village, with no prospects for the future.

One night, as the great North Wind came whistling through the woods, shaking the tiny cabin where they lived, an enormous white bear suddenly appeared at their door.

"Good evening," said the bear.

"Good evening," replied the man. Though he had not encountered a talking bear before, it was well-known in those parts that animals who spoke were enchanted. It was, in fact, a great honor to be addressed by such a creature.

The man's family hovered about the room gaping at the peculiar visitor, anxious to know what business had brought him to their humble cottage.

"I have come for your firstborn daughter," the bear announced without preamble. "If she will come away with me, she will have everything she wishes for, and, what's more, I will make you and the rest of your family as rich as you are now poor."

Beguiled by the words of the white bear, the eldest daughter pleaded with her mother and father to let her go—for her parents were against it, insisting that it would bring bad luck on them to give up their daughter for wealth. But at last they relented, as the young woman would not be denied the adventure.

Packing took no amount of time, since the poor girl owned nearly nothing in the world, and bravely she kissed each member of her family goodbye and climbed onto the back of the huge white bear. She barely had time for one last backward glance at her family before she was abruptly whisked away, with extraordinary speed, to a large white castle. There, servants rushed to and fro to attend to her arrival. Everything happened so quickly that she could scarcely take in her extravagant surroundings, and all of a sudden she felt terribly afraid. What was to become of her?

Perceiving her anxiety, the bear instructed a kindly old servant woman to take the girl to her bedchamber. But before she left him he advised her not to be afraid, assuring her that the castle was indeed enchanted and that, for as long as she remained there, all of her innermost desires would be immediately brought about. He handed her a little golden bell, adding that if, in fact, the castle failed in this tall order, all she had to do was to ring the bell while wishing for anything within the castle walls, and it would be immediately done for her. Then, with a polite bow, the bear left her with the old servant woman, who chattered away amicably as she led the girl to her bedchamber. What the servant spoke about she could not have said, so preoccupied was she, but the old lady's sociable manner had the effect of calming her nerves.

Inside her bedchamber, she first noticed the bed, a massive furnishing of elaborately carved mahogany dressed in lavish silks. Next she spied a dressing table, as splendidly adorned as the bed and laid out with solid-gold utensils for her to use.

At one end of the chamber there stood a series of wardrobes, each so large that it exceeded, in size, the entire bedroom she had formerly shared with all of her siblings back in her father's cottage. The wardrobes were stocked with beautiful gowns of many styles and colors, all of which were made to fit her just so. She selected a nightgown that was finer than any item of clothing she had ever before possessed and, wondering how the rest of her family had fared, she settled into the comfortable bedding that had been prepared just for her.

Her previous anxiety was for the most part gone now, but upon laying her head on the velvety pillow, she was overcome with a feeling of restlessness. Everything was so perfect and yet she felt a strange emptiness and longing.

Was she homesick? No, for although she loved her family, she was of an age when the solitude of private rooms, with her own possessions, was more than welcome! Besides, she could remember feeling this way in her father's cottage, too. Back then she had thought it was simply discontent, brought about by her passionate desire for nicer things, but here was the sensation again, stronger than ever, even among such incredible luxury and wealth. She still suffered with that same yearning, without knowing exactly what it was she wanted.

Before she had time to consider this at any great length, the door to her bedchamber abruptly opened and closed, and she heard someone enter her room. She had extinguished the candle, and no moon or starlight could creep through the thick velvet curtains that covered the windows, so she was completely unable to observe who it was.

She was not immediately alarmed, however, supposing that it was only the kindly servant woman, returning to tuck her in for the night or, perhaps, even, perceiving her unspoken and melancholy longing, the woman had duly fetched the vague thing and promptly brought it to her! For hadn't the bear promised that her every wish would be immediately granted?

But there was none of the servant's silly chattering this time; no, not even an answer when the girl inquired, "Who is it, please?"

She slowly sat up in the bed and instinctively turned her head toward the intruder, straining to detect the meaning of the soft shuffling sounds she now heard. As she stared into the blackness her eyes opened wider. Their sightless orbs darted back and forth in sudden terror.

At length it occurred to her that the trespasser had undressed. Then she heard someone approach the bed. She was hardly able to breathe, she was so terrified, but she somehow managed to whisper, "Who is it?"

Still the stranger said nothing.

"Who is it?" she repeated, more frantically. "Is it you, Mr. Bear?" But even as she asked this, she realized it could not be so, for the bear did not wear clothes or shoes, as had this uninvited visitor.

The question was once again ignored as, very leisurely, the stranger sat upon the bed. She was now certain that it could not be the huge white bear, for the personage who sat next to her on the bed was the precise size of a man. She had seen no men in the castle (every servant she had encountered was a woman), and so she had no clues as to his identity.

She began to disentangle her legs from inside the bedding,

thinking to bolt from the bed, when suddenly a hand reached out and gently grasped hold of her hair.

She gasped and repeated her request. "Please tell me who you are!"

Tightening his grip on her hair, the man carefully wound it around his hand slowly, round and round, until he reached her scalp. Then he gently pulled his hand downward, forcing her head and body back down on the bed and underneath him. Thus he held her head firmly as his lips approached hers.

"It is I," he replied in a soft whisper, lightly brushing her lips with his as he spoke. "Your lover, beckoned."

In the next instant his lips were pressing gently against hers, opening her mouth. His warm lips and probing tongue seemed to answer a calling from somewhere deep within her. She was astounded by her body's immediate response to him.

Even so, the thought of a complete stranger holding her thus filled her with horror. He lifted his mouth from hers and began soft gentle kisses along the line of her jaw.

"I must know who you are," she murmured. "The bear…"

"I am the reason you are here," he whispered between kisses. "And you—you are the reason I am here."

"But…" She had so many questions, but his mouth once again silenced her.

From his position over her and the way in which he held her, she knew that he was a large, muscular man. He smelled of shaving cream and light cologne. His hair was still damp from his bath. But who was he?

His kiss was so intense that she wasn't even conscious at first that she was kissing him back. A warm feeling trickled up from deep within her womb. She tried to hold on to logic and reason.

"Please," she begged, "light a lantern that I might at least see you."

But he neither answered her plea nor permitted the light. He merely continued to devour her lips and flushed skin. Although his body was covering hers, he held himself up slightly so that his weight would not crush her. Still, he remained close enough that she could feel him hardening above her. Her own desire was rapidly becoming a stronger force in her surrender than his hold on her hair.

She reached out her hand in an attempt to touch his face, thinking that she might at least feel his features with her fingers, but he gently brushed her hand away and continued to kiss her. His breath was warm and pleasant.

Fragments of the last few hours whirled around in her consciousness. The stranger, who had appeared so suddenly, said that each of them was the reason for the other being there. And she could not forget the words of the bear, promising that the enchanted castle would bring about her every desire. But she only vaguely remembered the strange yearnings she had been feeling when the stranger came to her room, for they had all but disappeared upon his arrival!

Was it her own desire, then, that had brought this stranger to her? Wasn't he, in fact, doing things that she had always wished someone would do? But who was he? Was he even real, or just a figment of her imagination? Oh, but it was impossible to think with him kissing her! His lips were insistent and enticing, and she began to feel herself giving in to a fate that, uncertain as it was, was infinitely more pleasant than any other she had encountered in her meager life so far.

A new, warmer longing was rising up from within her. She wanted his kisses to go on forever, but at length she became aware that he was reaching beneath her nightgown. He placed his warm hand on her stomach for a moment, allowing her to become accustomed to his touch. Slowly and gently he began to move his hand, exploring her body carefully and thoroughly, and ultimately leaving every part of her that he touched yearning when he abandoned it for another. His other hand still held her hair in its grasp, preventing escape, though her desire to escape had abated. In fact, her arms, seemingly of their own accord, wound themselves around his neck, and her lips began uttering soft sounds that were unintelligible to both of them.

The stranger carefully released his hold on her hair.

He once again placed his lips on hers as he slowly and carefully peeled the edges of her nightgown down over her shoulders and torso and legs. With her fully exposed to his hands, he began to caress her more earnestly, feeling every inch of her from head to foot, as if attempting to see her through his touch. She trembled beneath him as he slowly and meticulously continued his intimate examination, seemingly fascinated by every little curve and indentation. She didn't wonder about his reaction to what he discovered, for she could feel his own rigid body against hers throughout his administrations.

But he was in no hurry, regardless of his growing excitement, and his very adept fingers gradually gave way to an even more skillful tongue. Clutching the extravagant bedding in her hands, she felt herself submitting completely under her mystery lover's captivating seduction.

Meanwhile the stranger's strong hands held her firmly as he continued to rouse her with his tongue. She nearly fainted from the pleasure he was giving her, and just when she felt that something within her very core would certainly burst, he raised himself over her and positioned her limbs to accommodate his larger form.

But she struggled against him in sudden panic as it once again occurred to her that she had no knowledge of who this man was. He paused and held back, unwilling to take her by force. With her whole being tremulous with desire, she desperately reached out her hands in another attempt to touch his face but, even in the dark, he easily intercepted her wrists and held them firmly over her head to prevent any further efforts to discover his identity.

Being thus laid open and pinned, her fears seemed pointless, especially while her body was overcome with such an intense craving for the man, whoever he was. He kissed her lips very tenderly, as if to make amends for the unrelenting hold he maintained on her hands, and she wrapped her legs around his torso, at last giving him the consent he had been waiting for.

His kiss suddenly became rougher as he abruptly thrust himself into her willing body. Her head turned away from him in a reflexive movement as she stared mutely into the blackness that surrounded them, momentarily overcome by the many sensations that were flooding through her. But in the next heartbeat, she turned back toward him and received his lips anxiously, breathing his warm breath and tasting his tongue with her own.

Giving herself completely now to her unknown lover, she began to respond, moving her body to enhance the extreme pleasure he was giving her. Longing to hold him, but unable to use her arms, which were still detained by his grasp, she clung to him with her legs. They continued in this way long into the night, until at last, they both lay quiet and sedate.

On the following morning she woke up alone, and try as

she might, she could not find a single man within the walls of the castle that day. Instead she discovered many different rooms—rooms that were filled with rich fabrics of every material and style; rooms containing shelves upon shelves of thread and yarn of every single thickness and shade; rooms containing baskets of varying shapes and sizes; rooms for growing flowers; one room was filled with every kind of button that had ever been made. In short, for every occupation the lady could ever wish to engage in, there was a room filled with a wide variety of materials for that craft.

And so it was that, although the young woman was obliged to pass each day in her own company, she nevertheless had everything she could wish for to interest her. And each night her mysterious lover came to lie beside her in the dark, always leaving before daylight, so that she never once caught a single glimpse of him. Weeks came and went in this way and, although she came to love the nights, she began to tire of the isolated days, in spite of the variety of materials that had been provided for her amusement.

One day, recalling the words of the white bear when she first came to the castle, she rang the little golden bell and wished to see the bear. He immediately appeared. But she was unsure of how to proceed.

"Who," she began cautiously, "is the master of this castle?"

"It is I," replied he.

She was silent for a moment. She longed to ask him for information about the man who came to her each night, but it occurred to her that her lover might have deceived her about the white bear. Perhaps the bear would be angered by the discovery of their nightly intimacies. Oh, how she wished her mother were there to advise her!

This thought gave her a new idea, and she asked the bear

if he would take her to visit her family. The bear immediately agreed, upon condition.

"Soon after you arrive," he warned, "your mother will try to take you aside and speak with you privately. Avoid doing so or you will bring bad luck upon us both."

The girl was reluctant to agree to this condition, for a private interview with her mother was precisely what she wanted. But finally she consented, as she was now anxious to see her family, and thought perhaps there would come another way to find the answers she sought.

Servants were immediately called upon to pack her bags, and then she was once again whisked away on the back of the white bear. In a very short time they appeared before a huge mansion.

"You have arrived," the bear told her. "This is where your family lives now."

She was very pleased by this, and hurried to be with them. But the bear held her back a moment longer with the stern admonition, "Heed my warning! Do not go off alone with your mother, or it will fare badly for us both."

Hers was a happy homecoming indeed, with none of them wanting for anything, and she did not forget her promise to the white bear. As the bear predicted, her mother made many attempts to get her alone, but each of these she managed to elude.

But her mother was not to be easily put off, and finally that persistent lady succeeded in arranging a private interview between herself and her daughter, where she posed many questions to find out how things really were in the castle of the white bear. It was not long before the girl had confided in her mother about the mysterious man that entered her bedchamber each night.

Her mother was deeply alarmed by all her daughter said and, giving her a candle, instructed her to take it with her on her return to the castle and hide it beneath her pillow.

"When the stranger is asleep, light the candle that you might learn his identity," her mother instructed her. But she added, "Take care not to tip the candle, letting the tallow fall upon him."

With this advice the young woman journeyed back to the castle, hiding the candle amongst her belongings.

Evening came soon enough, and it was the same as it had been before; as soon as the darkness enveloped her bedchamber, her anonymous lover came to her. She had missed him while she was away and longed for his touch in the darkened chamber. He did not leave her waiting, for he had yearned for her also during her absence.

As a lover, she knew him well, and yet she still wondered whose tongue it was that tasted her lips. Whose hot breath seared her delicate skin? Whose strong and nimble fingers stroked and explored the many soft and hidden places of her body, and whose unyielding arms held her in their strong grip? Whose body filled her so completely, in so many ways, and with such violent frenzy?

And still, she could not hold back from participating wholeheartedly, dubious though it was.

At last her lover slept beside her. She felt under her pillow for the candle she had placed there earlier and, disregarding the bear's warnings about bad luck, lit the candle and placed it before the stranger's face. There she beheld the most beautiful prince she had ever dared to imagine, and she immediately fell so deeply in love with him that she felt she must kiss him that very instant. She bent over him to gently touch her lips to his and, as she did so, a drop from the burning candle fell onto his chest. He immediately awoke, demanding, "What have you done?"

The lovesick girl could not fathom his displeasure until he explained that he was indeed a prince, who had been promised at birth to marry a princess whom he did not love. When he refused the marriage, his stepmother had placed an evil curse on him, wherein he would appear as a white bear by day, and return to his human form by night. His only chance to escape the unwanted marriage and the curse was to remain unseen by his true love for an entire year.

"Now I must go to the castle that is east of the sun and west of the moon, and marry the dreadful princess," he told her.

She wept bitterly when she heard this, but neither tears nor pleading could change their fate, and they spent that evening clinging miserably to each other in the dark.

The next morning the wretched lady woke up alone. The castle and the prince had both disappeared. The only thing that remained was the little bundle of rags that she had brought with her on her very first journey there. She cried until every tear she possessed was lost forever.

"I must find him and get him back," she decided at last. But where was the castle that was east of the sun and west of the moon?

She picked up her bundle and set out on the nearest road. After traveling only a short distance she came upon an old woman sitting by the roadside. She asked the ragged-looking woman if she knew how to get to the castle that was east of the sun and west of the moon.

"Are you the true love of the prince from there?" asked the woman knowingly.

"Why yes," replied the startled girl. "Do you know the way there?"

"No," cackled the hag, thinking it a great joke. But then she added more kindly, "Take this golden apple, it may be of use to you in your travels."

So the girl took the golden apple from the woman and continued down the road. In a short time she chanced to meet another old woman on the side of the road. This one she also approached for directions to the castle.

"You must be the true love of the prince," the old woman surmised, just as the other had.

"I am she," owned the girl. "Please can't you tell me the way to his castle?"

But this old woman could offer no more information on the location of the prince's castle than the other. She gave the girl an enchanted hair comb, instructing her to wear it if she found the prince, as it would bring her good luck to do so.

With still not the slightest idea of how to find her prince, the heartbroken girl continued doggedly on and, at length, met with yet another old woman along the road. With this woman she shared a similar exchange as she had with the other two. This woman advised her to seek the East Wind for the information she desired and, giving her a magic feather, instructed her to thrust it out before her and follow it to the home of the East Wind.

Accordingly the girl tossed the magic feather out in front of her, which was immediately picked up by a strong wind that came from the west. Following the magic feather, she now made much better time and quickly found herself at the doorstep of the east wind. Her journey was far from over however; for the east wind knew not the location of the castle that lay east of the sun and west of the moon. So he took her to his brother, the west wind, who took her to see the south wind, until finally it was determined that the north wind was the only one who could help her after all.

And so, after many days and nights of travel and much hardship, she hopped on the wings of the north wind and was on her way to the castle that lay east of the sun and west of the moon.

When the North Wind at last dropped her at the entrance of the long-searched-for castle, she was a frightful sight and, try as she might, she could not gain entrance there. Frustrated, she sat under a large window to think of what she could try next. Unconsciously, she began to play with the golden apple that was given to her by the first old woman on the roadside. She repeatedly tossed the apple into the air, catching it as it came down.

Now the prince's evil stepmother caught sight of her playing with the golden apple from her window high above. The greedy woman instantly resolved to have the rare treasure and offered the girl anything she wished in exchange for it.

"I wish to see my true love, the prince," announced the girl boldly.

The prince's stepmother was taken aback by this audacious reply but allowed the girl inside so that she might ultimately find a way to get the apple from her.

"If indeed you are the true love of my stepson, the prince," began his crafty caretaker, "then you could no doubt pick him from one hundred men."

"Of course," replied the girl.

"Well then, in that case, I shall grant you an opportunity to pick your true love from among one hundred men, in exchange for that golden apple."

"Gladly," agreed the girl, holding out the apple, but then as an afterthought, she added, "of course, I will also need a bath and a new dress."

The stepmother agreed to her conditions with a wicked laugh, snatching the apple from her, and then quickly ringing a bell to summon a servant. Dismissing the girl to the care of the servant, she wandered off to gloat over her treasure.

The prince's true love was bathed in scented water and then given a beautiful golden gown to wear. Remembering, suddenly, the words of the second old woman by the roadside, she swept her hair up in the enchanted hair comb.

When these preparations were completed, she followed the servant to the dining room. But upon arriving there she found herself in an empty room, with only one place setting on the table. A handsome young manservant entered, bringing her an assortment of delicious treats for dinner.

"Am I not to dine with the prince?" she asked him.

"After dinner, madam, you will be brought before the prince and allowed to choose him...or any other that you wish." He said this civilly enough, but with such a smirk on his face that she drew back as if she had been slapped.

"I have come a very far distance to find my prince," she replied haughtily. "I can't imagine why you would dare to imply that I might choose another man besides him!"

"Perhaps it was wishful thinking" was his rejoinder. "You see, I am one of the other ninety-nine men you will be choosing from."

"I do see," she replied curtly, thinking to herself, *You will be punished for your impertinence when I marry the prince!* She ate what she could of the dinner in silence.

Shortly after the meal, she was led to the room where she would at last see her beloved prince. The servant left her at the door. Taking a deep breath, she opened it. There stood the prince's stepmother.

"Where is the prince?" demanded the frustrated girl.

"He is just beyond that door," his stepmother replied, pointing to yet another door at the far end of the room.

"But," she added, just as the girl was rushing toward that portal, "there are a few things you should know before you rush in there." She smiled as she continued. "There are one hundred men in that room. All of them have been placed under a spell so that they cannot move from the place where they stand, and they cannot utter a sound. It was necessary to do this, for, if you truly love the prince, you must find him among the men without his help."

"I do not need to hear him speak to find him, nor will he be required to come to me," replied the girl.

"Also," continued the stepmother, ignoring her remark and smiling wider, "since you strengthened the original curse by bringing light upon the darkness, you must now relinquish the light and once again enter the darkness to find and save your beloved prince."

The girl gasped. "Do you mean to say that I must distinguish him from ninety-nine others—in the dark?"

"If it is really true love, it can be done," the cruel woman replied, again dismissing the girl by ringing the servant's bell. But before leaving the girl alone, she turned to add, "Be careful to whom you speak in the room, for your choice of a 'true love' will be determined by the first man you speak to." And she was gone.

The girl turned to the servant who answered the bell, an older woman who regarded her kindly. "I should be grateful if you could offer any advice," she implored.

"Remove your clothes," said the old woman calmly.

"What!" exclaimed the girl.

"Remove your clothes," repeated the woman. "That is how you know him and you will choose the man you know."

"But, what if…" she paused, uncertain.

"It is the only way," replied the shrewd old woman. "You will not get another chance after this."

Seeing the wisdom in the old woman's words, she quickly removed her clothing. Then she opened the door and walked into the blackness beyond. The door closed immediately behind her.

Although the room was silent, she could feel the presence of the men who crowded the large room. Slowly she moved forward. It occurred to her suddenly that she hadn't even touched the face of her prince, for he had thwarted her every attempt to seek his identity. She had only that one glimpse of him by candlelight. She knew him only as a lover. Would that be enough to help her now?

All of a sudden, she felt someone beside her. She reached out her hand in the dark and discovered a man standing there. The thought of the smirking servant crossed her mind, and she recoiled instantly. But the man reached out a steady hand and held her. With her heart racing, she let him draw her near. His hands slid down the length of her body, touching her intimately. She tried to concentrate on his hands and recall exactly how her prince's hands had felt when they were touching her. Were these his hands that caressed her now? The man reached a hand between her legs, prying her open and thrusting a finger inside her warm body.

But something was wrong. The fingers that were digging into her flesh were cold, not warm like her lover's. With a small cry of horror, she tore herself from the impostor's hands.

The next man she encountered had much warmer hands.

Like the former, he touched her body intimately, without reserve. Did all men grasp and clutch at a woman in exactly the same manner?

But there seemed to be something familiar in this one's touch. She turned up her face towards his in the darkness. His lips immediately came down on hers in a soft kiss. Pressing her body close to his, she slowly wound her arms around his neck, thinking this man could be her prince. Her body began responding to his warm kisses and caresses, and yet, a slow dawning crept up within her that this man could not be her prince after all, for his kisses were much too wet!

And so it was that, as she went up and down the length of the room, she searched in vain for her prince. There were indeed a few times when she believed she might have found him, but in her fear of choosing the wrong man she always held back from speaking. Yet she clung to those men who reminded her of the one she loved and, yes, even allowed a few of them to take her, right there in the room, thinking that she had at last found her prince, only to discover moments later that he could not have been him after all.

Her whole body shook with frustration and anxiety over the enormity of the task that lay before her. She was in a constant state of arousal as she wandered about the room, doing unimaginable things with complete strangers. And as the night wore on, she could not determine one touch from the next, but only hoped for a miraculous sign that would enlighten her and free her from the degrading search she had been forced to endure. And all the while she knew that her prince was there, silently listening to her moans and cries as she traversed the room, and perceiving her inability to quit the arms of each impostor before giving a little bit of herself to him.

Tears poured down her cheeks as she pressed on, discouraged, but unable to give up until she found him. She wondered if she had encountered the servant from the dining room yet, and if so, how far she had allowed him to go with her. Was he one of the men who had taken her right there on the floor, easing the aching hunger she felt, if only for the moment?

Blindly she stumbled on, praying for a miracle. And there, in front of her, stood yet another man. She approached him with the tears still on her cheeks.

Abruptly the man clutched her in a fierce embrace and crushed her lips under his. She could not remember having ever been kissed so violently and struggled to get away from the savage grasp that was bruising her skin. He did not relent, however, and she almost cried out for help, but at that same moment she remembered that she could not speak. If she spoke out she would not only lose her prince forever, but possibly be obliged to remain with this brute as well! A real terror seized her, as she realized that the violent stranger might force himself on her, without her even being able to utter a single word.

But the man seemed to collect himself and he loosened his hold somewhat, although not enough so that she could escape him. For several moments he simply held her close to him, and she could feel his heart hammering inside his chest. His face was buried in her hair and, momentarily mesmerized by the smell of it; he relaxed his hold on her slightly as he inhaled the sweet scent.

Thinking this her opportunity to bolt, she twisted herself out of his grasp and turned to flee. In that instant, the enchanted comb fell from her hair, releasing it, even as her captor reached out for her. Her loosened tresses fell directly into one of his hands and he closed it tightly around them. She was abruptly obliged to halt her escape.

Very slowly, and purposefully, he wound her hair around his

hand, round and round, bringing her closer and closer to him, until her face was only inches from his own. Something within her stirred. With his hand still clutching her hair, he gently pulled backwards, forcing her head back and positioning her lips directly below his own. She felt his familiar warm breath on her lips before he claimed them in a gentle kiss, just like the old familiar kisses she now remembered. She shuddered to think that she had almost run away from him. But why had he been so violent with her when she first approached him?

She blushed suddenly as she imagined her prince standing there in the dark, listening to the sounds of her lovemaking with those impostors who managed to fool her into thinking that they were him. She realized that it was anger that had made him grab her so brutally.

But he was tender with her now, as his body entered her right there where he was obliged to stand until she released him. They clung to each other in the darkness and, finally certain of her true prince, she whispered, "I love you."

Upon this admission, they were at once returned to the castle of the white bear, where they were both once again lying together in their very own bed. There were one hundred candles lit about the room, and the two gazed at each other, amazed by all that had happened.

The prince and his true love were married, of course, and have lived happily together since that day. And though she loves nothing more than the sight of her handsome prince, his wife sometimes dreams about that unknown lover, and, on such occasions, he comes to her.

Even now, this very evening, the prince is waiting outside her bedchamber door until it is fully dark, when he will slip quietly in…

Goldilocks and
the Three Barons

There is little that is so utterly vexing as an interfering busybody. Such a one is always poking about, seemingly trying to learn about causes and effects, but generally just stirring up a great deal of trouble over nothing. These meddlesome trespassers bash and barge their way into the most intimate places, disregarding decorum and logic in their efforts to create an illusion of something shocking or remarkable. It matters not whether the affair they are about to divulge is real or factual; either way it must be exposed. And one of the most notorious of these offenders was Goldilocks.

Goldilocks was deeply interested in matters not relating to her, particularly those of a confidential nature. These she would turn into feature articles that she would then submit to her editor at the *Woodland Enquirer*. She had exposed and humiliated countless inhabitants of the forest in just this way, and it was a dreadful thing, indeed, when one was unfortunate enough to have done something to capture her notice.

It was through this circumstance that Goldilocks came to be in a more remote part of the forest one morning, in search of three English barons who lived there. It was a curious and unusual thing to her that three men should decide to separate themselves from civilization and live alone together in the deepest part of the woods. Unconventional behavior, to her mind, was synonymous with wrongdoing, and since the men were wealthy and renowned, she felt it her responsibility to reveal their secrets to the world.

The barons, on the other hand, were completely unaware of the interest they had stirred with their actions. Although they were indeed isolated from the rest of society, living so far out in the country, the lifestyle nevertheless suited them, for they were pompous and intolerant by nature, and found the general community to be somewhat odious and tiresome. The common tastes of the majority were unbearably vulgar to them, and the general public's concerns seemed utterly absurd. In view of these opinions, it did not seem at all out of the ordinary to the barons that they should wish to separate themselves from what they considered to be the lower classes. And, in truth, these supposed lower classes were no doubt better off for not having shared a more intimate acquaintance with the snooty barons.

And so it was, with their usual self-absorption and total unawareness of any interests outside of their own, that the barons sat down to eat their morning meal. Their only immediate concern was the observation that their morning porridge was unusually hot. A discussion ensued to determine a solution to the matter.

"I say," remarked the first baron, raising his eyebrows and

addressing his friends in an icy tone. "This porridge is exceedingly hot."

"Indeed," agreed the next. "It is offensive, to say the very least."

"Perhaps we should leave it where it lies in its incorrigible heat," added the third. "In time, I think, it will rehabilitate to something much more palatable."

So saying, the three set out for a morning walk in the woods, where they leisurely wandered about, amusing themselves with anecdotes about the wildlife that dwelled there. The animals scampered about happily, unsuspecting of any insult in the barons' mocking innuendos.

While the barons were thus discharged, Goldilocks discovered their secluded cottage. As she was not often of the mind to address her subjects directly, she approached the house cautiously. Very stealthily, so as not to be discovered, she advanced toward the back of the cottage and peered into a window. This glimpse did not provide the verification she sought, however, so she proceeded to another window, and then another, until she was finally satisfied that the house was, for the moment, abandoned.

Goldilocks crept up to the front entryway and put her ear against the door. There was not a sound to be heard within. Next she ventured a timid knock, to which there was no response. She tentatively turned the doorknob and, delighted to find the door unlocked, she opened it up and poked her head inside. After a moment, she stepped into the house and closed the door behind her.

Once inside the cottage, Goldilocks immediately noticed the porridge, dished out in bowls upon the table. As she was unmindful of the offense she committed by entering the barons' cottage uninvited, it should not shock the reader that

Goldilocks would further impose by tasting their food, which was so carefully laid out that she imagined it must have been intended for a guest such as herself to eat. Indeed, it would have seemed downright rude not to have done so. Besides, one can learn quite a lot about persons by the food that they eat, she reasoned neatly. And so, without further thought or consideration over the matter, she seated herself before one of the bowls and lifted the spoon to her lips.

"Oh," she exclaimed, jerking back. "This is too hot!" She pulled out her notebook and jotted down a few words. Then she moved to the second bowl to taste of it. But she nearly choked on that one as well, remarking, "This is too cold." Again she scribbled in her notebook. But the third bowl was more to her liking, and she said, "This is just right!" She made another quick notation before finishing the contents of that bowl.

Having concluded her research in the kitchen, Goldilocks ventured into the living room. There she found three very different chairs. She sat on one of them and practically slid right off the seat. "My goodness, this is much too hard!" she exclaimed, making a few notes before she went on. She sat on another chair and nearly disappeared into the cushions. "This is too soft," she observed, recording her thoughts. But the third chair was very comfortable, and she said, "This is just right." But the chair was old and, with a low creaking noise it suddenly burst apart, tossing poor Goldilocks onto the hard wooden floor. Furiously she scribbled in her notebook.

Confident now that she had indeed stumbled upon a story of significance, Goldilocks continued her tour down a long hallway that led to a room with three beds in it. Without sparing a single thought for modesty, she plunked herself down on one of the beds.

"This is too hard," she complained, moving to the next bed after making a quick note. "This is too soft" was her opinion of the second bed, which she duly recorded. But once again, the third one was a charm and, as she lay in the bed writing down her observations, her eyelids drooped. In a matter of moments she had fallen asleep!

Now as Goldilocks was sleeping peacefully in the bed, the barons returned home from their walk. Their appetites were heightened by the exercise, and they hungrily approached their bowls of porridge. But in an instant they noticed that something was amiss.

"I say," announced the first baron, with his usual pretentious air. "It appears as if someone has been nipping at my porridge."

"How droll!" exclaimed the second. But then, noticing his own bowl of porridge, he gasped. "Oh, dear" was all he seemed able to manage.

"Someone has indeed been eating our porridge," reported the third. "For there is not a drop left in my bowl!"

Alarmed by this singular event, the barons immediately set out to see if anything else in their home had been molested. The minute they entered the living room they noticed their chairs in disarray.

"Someone has been sitting in my chair," claimed the first, though no visible mark had been left on the hard wooden chair.

"Ditto for mine," assented the second, who stared without comprehension at the imprints left by Goldilocks's buttocks on the soft cushions.

"But what of my chair?" stormed the third. "It has been broken to bits!"

The three now advanced warily into the bedroom. The first

baron gasped when he saw the crumpled blankets on his bed. "Someone has been sleeping in my bed!" he announced.

"Someone has been sleeping in my bed," echoed the second.

"Someone has been sleeping in my bed, and she's still there!" declared the third, utterly astounded by this turn of events.

The high-pitched tone of this last remark startled Goldilocks awake. You can imagine her shock to see the three barons towering over her! She immediately jumped up, with the intention of making her escape through an open window, but the baron whose bed she had been sleeping in held her fast.

"Who are you, and why are you sleeping in my bed?" he asked her in an imperious tone.

"I'm Goldilocks," she replied. But of course she had no explanation for being in the baron's bed.

"You've eaten my porridge, broken my chair and messed up the blankets on my bed," continued the baron, looking her up and down with an expression of utter disdain. He held her with two fingers, while the remaining three fingers stood up at an angle as if to avoid contamination. "Hold still while I contact the authorities!"

"Oh, no!" cried Goldilocks. "You cannot do that." She was still trying to work her way out of the last legal dispute that had developed over her disreputable journalistic ethics. Even her editor would not be able to help her out of this one!

The baron seemed genuinely perplexed by her outburst. "Cannot I?" he asked. "But why ever not?" He looked at his friends quizzically, but they only returned his puzzled stare, unable to provide a logical reason why he could not call the authorities.

"Because I have been expressly assigned to come here!" lied Goldilocks hastily, struggling frantically to come up with a plausible excuse for her actions, preferably one that would keep her from being sued again.

"Expressly assigned?" repeated the baron, more confused than ever. It never occurred to him that he was being bamboozled. "Under whose employ were you expressly assigned to come here, and for what reason?"

"Well…um," Goldilocks tried to think of a quick answer.

"I bet it was Count Wallingford!" spoke up one of the other barons suddenly. "Don't you remember the hoax we played on him last winter?"

They all looked at Goldilocks in wonder. She smiled, attempting to look like she had been found out, grasping at the baron's suggestion without understanding his meaning.

"He did vow that he would return the favor," recalled the first.

"Oh, my, what a perfectly scandalous idea!" exclaimed the third baron. But he said this with such glee that one could not really believe he was terribly scandalized.

"Indeed," remarked the baron who had threatened to call the authorities only moments before. He now lightened his grip on Goldilocks and smiled broadly as he contemplated the situation. "But where on earth do you suppose he managed to find such a trollop?"

"We must ask him the next time we see him," said his friend with a chuckle, but their demeanor and attitude were quickly changing, and they were at once more jovial and good-humored. They moved in closer to Goldilocks and, very leisurely, began unbuttoning her dress. As they did so, they spoke to one another cheerfully, paying little attention to Goldilocks as they made blunt observations about her clothing.

"Upon my word," remarked the first, as he pulled the dress over her head and held it up to his friends. "Of what sort of material is this ungainly rag made?"

"I can't say that I have ever encountered anything like it before," replied the second, wrinkling his nose with a look of distaste. "It reminds one of the stuff used to hold potatoes!"

"Indeed," chuckled the third, taking perverse delight in its shabbiness. "I half expected to find some of that product upon your removing the thing."

"Oh, but you must see these!" screeched the first baron. He tugged at Goldilocks's undergarments, barely acknowledging her at all as he nearly ripped them off her body and held them up to his friends. "Why, they are absolutely revolting!"

His friends gasped in horror at the sight of the cotton pantaloons, so unlike the silken undergarments they were used to seeing in the stores where they shopped.

Goldilocks stared at them in astonishment. Before she had the presence of mind to comprehend their intentions she was standing naked before them, watching mutely as they nonchalantly discussed her clothing. Next, they began to undress themselves, doing so in a very casual and unhurried manner, carefully folding each article of clothing as they removed it and placing it neatly over a chair. At last the first baron laid himself across the bed that Goldilocks had been sleeping in only a few moments before. He raised his eyebrows and looked at her expectantly.

"Well?" he said, and when she only stared at him he tapped the bed, exclaiming, "Look alive, old girl!"

The other two, meanwhile, led her to where he lay. To her utter bewilderment, she could not bring herself to resist. It was most certainly her excessive curiosity that had brought her to this point, and now it once again pushed her onward to see the outcome of this unusual but exciting episode. To the barons, she was a total stranger who had been procured to entertain them. They would most likely never discover her real identity, so she could walk away from the experience as if it had never happened, and yet with a new knowledge of herself and the world around her. She had never before been presented with such an opportunity, and likely would not again. Aside from all of this, she felt herself to be under some queer influence, so that she could not oppose the oddly authoritative will of the barons, or this most peculiar orgy.

The two barons guided Goldilocks so that she was positioned on top of the first baron just so, but she gasped suddenly, saying, "This is too hard!"

To this the baron replied, "That will be remedied in a short while."

Accepting this, Goldilocks allowed herself to be placed fully upon him, and immediately an intense pleasure shot through her as she was obliged, in this position, to take every bit of his hardness inside of her.

The second baron positioned himself directly in front of Goldilocks's face and summoned her to open her lips. "This is too soft," she could not help remarking just before he stuffed himself into her mouth.

"That, too, will be remedied without delay," replied he. And within seconds of having said so, Goldilocks realized that he had spoken the truth.

Goldilocks now glanced sideways at the third baron as he saturated himself with some kind of lubricant. "Oh," she thought, "that is just right." But she reconsidered this in the next instant, for he had positioned himself directly behind her—and it did not immediately feel "just right" where he was forcing himself into her from behind. She gasped.

Thus engaged, Goldilocks felt something like a butterfly might, when the collector methodically spreads apart its wings and firmly fastens it to his exhibit. And while it is true that the barons had almost as little regard for Goldilocks as the collector has for his butterfly, she had their concentrated attention for the moment at least, and the desire they felt for her was unmistakable. As for Goldilocks, her every sense was alive with feeling; yet, pinioned as she was, she was completely immobilized and absolutely vulnerable to their will.

The barons stroked and fondled every part of Goldilocks as they took her, meanwhile groaning under the strain to go slow; for they were determined to enjoy every aspect of this little windfall that had blown in their direction. With this in mind, they, in turns, went fast and slow, making full use of her eager body.

Meanwhile, Goldilocks could feel her own excitement pressing up within her. She had never felt so overwhelmed and, at the same time, so desperate for more. She gasped and whimpered when the barons became more demanding, relentlessly driving into her with a force that matched her own excitement. But ere long, they would once again slow the pace, forcing themselves to hold back in an effort to prolong the experience, and at these intervals they would devote themselves to touching her face, hair, breasts, and buttocks. Often they would comment on her physical appearance, noting such things as the softness of her skin, or the roundness of her buttocks, or the eagerness of her mouth. Hearing them, Goldilocks became overcome with desire, and suddenly wanted to be used by them—even more shamefully so.

She spread her legs wider and arched her back, pushing her hips upward and forcing herself to take the third baron completely in her backside. The discomfort this caused mingled with her pleasure and gave her the fuel she needed to reach her ultimate pleasure.

Alternately she pressed herself against the first baron, moving forward and backward on him so that he, too, received an equal turn of pleasure. Not wanting to neglect the second baron, she opened her mouth wider and tipped back her head, so that he could push himself farther into her throat, and with each thrust she felt an exquisite thrill to her very core.

All of these efforts she made were duly noted and remarked upon by the barons, and their comments added fuel to the fire that was burning hotter and deeper within her, threatening to consume her.

Goldilocks was responding to the barons in earnest now, caressing each one with that part of her body he possessed. She cared not how she appeared or how they would remember her later, for, to the extent that she pleased them, to that extent she felt her own pleasure. Her body gyrated wildly as she choked out sounds of pleasure. The barons watched her with admiration and delight, and marveled that she not only yielded to them, but also seemed to want them to use her more harshly.

Holding back their climax repeatedly, the three barons intended to employ Goldilocks's body for as long as she would allow it. The baron who had her mouth held her by her golden locks, pulling her hair this way and that, according to the position he desired her mouth to be in. The baron beneath her held her breasts in both hands, pinching the nipples fiercely while she shuddered and wriggled helplessly on top of his body. The third baron slapped her backside brutally, much like he would have done to his horse if it did not please him.

But finally the barons could delay their excitement no longer, and they each became more urgent, roughly thrusting themselves into her body. Their crude use of her sent Goldilocks over the edge, and she cried out screams of pleasure as her body finally reached a most glorious release. That was the breaking point for the barons, and they lost all control, loudly filling her body to overflowing.

A few moments later Goldilocks once again found herself back in the same woods where she had begun her day. She pondered distractedly over what had happened to her. If not for the telltale soreness throughout her body she would have fancied the whole thing was no more than a daydream. But she knew it was no daydream, and she wondered over what she had done and how it had all come about.

"Was it wrong of me to venture into the barons' cottage uninvited?" she questioned. "But no. If it were wrong, I surely would not have been so thoroughly rewarded!"

And so, poor Goldilocks learned nothing from her experience, and will no doubt continue to intrude and trespass into the private affairs of others. But as for you and me, we shall not be so reckless, and I daresay that we will be especially careful to avoid any strange, masculine cottages we happen to find isolated in the deepest part of the woods.

Or will we?

Mirror on the Wall

Once upon a time, in a kingdom known far and wide for its beautiful women, there lived a sorcerer who fell in love with one of the maidens who dwelt there. This maiden was untrue to the sorcerer, however, and shortly afterward, he died of a broken heart. With his last breath he cast a spell upon the entire kingdom and, for all I know, it remains there to this day.

Under the spell of the broken-hearted sorcerer, all the women of this kingdom suddenly appeared unfamiliar and disagreeable to their male counterparts and even to themselves. They immediately began a campaign to become the exact opposite of what nature intended them to be. First, they starved themselves almost to death, because this emaciated condition was thought to be more appealing than the normal womanly appearance that came from being healthy. Those who could not withstand this deprivation submitted to other humiliating methods of ridding themselves of the unwanted flesh. Next, their breasts had to be altered from their natural shape to a larger, stiffer prototype, which, though causing much pain and many health problems, had a more desirable effect for everyone. Aging was the most detestable of all the natural manifestations in women, and it was to be avoided at all costs. Women did everything in their power to prevent it, finally succumbing to dangerous medical procedures when all else failed.

Although such an existence may seem far-fetched and improbable to many a reader, I can assure you, it is quite true. One could not expound too earnestly on the lengths to which these poor creatures were willing to go in their efforts to be anything besides that which they were. Why, even the hair upon their heads and bodies was incomprehensible to them, so that they cut, curled, colored, plucked, waxed, shaved and electrocuted until every single strand was either altered or destroyed.

The few women who managed to fit into this uncomfortable mode of expectation were given the status of queen—for a short while—during which time they were expected to exploit themselves for the pleasure of men, and for the punishment of the women who were not complying as properly as it was believed they ought.

In short, an intense misery came over the female inhabitants of this accursed land.

Now it came to pass that a certain woman of beauty, even for those times, happened to be nearing her time to expire; that is to say, she was approaching the age when her value as a woman and queen, according to the standards under the spell, was nearing its end. The soon-to-be-former queen frantically searched the books and leaflets that were published to advise the women of her kingdom, but, finding no comfort or guidance that would suffice, she at last found herself standing before an immense mirror that hung ominously over her on a wall in her bedchamber. In a state of despair, she cried:

"Mirror, mirror, on the wall;
How much longer 'til I fall.
Was my beauty all in vain?
Or can you help to ease my pain?"

Now, the mirrors, along with the women's publications throughout this land were under the curse of the evil spell; they were, in fact, the very conduits through which the spell gained strength and power.

The mirror, therefore, had been patiently waiting for this opportunity, and now replied:

"Your beauty, once beyond compare,
Soon will be no longer there.
You must find one like you once were,
Take and eat the heart of her!"

The queen gasped in horror at the words the mirror spoke, which continued to echo faintly throughout her bedchamber. *Take and eat the heart of her!* How ghastly (and most definitely fattening), she thought. She peered more closely into the glass. There she spied two tiny lines that had settled themselves comfortably below each of her gaping eyes. She flung herself from the mirror with a screech.

Take and eat the heart of her!

Unable to endure the mirror a moment longer, the queen flew from her bedchamber. Suddenly she came face-to-face with her stepdaughter, who was called Snow White because her skin was as clear and pure as newly fallen snow. The queen had never been particularly fond of her stepdaughter—for in those times women were rarely fond of other females, even in the child form—but she had been tolerant of her up until now in memory of Snow White's father.

On this occasion, however, the queen could not help but notice the extraordinary beauty of Snow White, and it occurred to her that the tiresome child had grown up to be almost as beautiful as she herself had once been. *Find one like you once were.* The queen shuddered as she recalled the mirror's words, and she immediately sent Snow White away from her to labor in the kitchen.

And so, for a time, life went on in this manner, with poor Snow White forced to act as a servant in her father's house, and her stepmother, the queen, in such a state of dejection that she could not look upon Snow White without feeling physical pain.

One morning, as the queen's expiration date was getting perilously near, the unfortunate woman once again found herself standing before the large mirror in her bedchamber. Soon she was uttering the same pitiful plea:

"Mirror, mirror, on the wall.
How much longer 'til I fall?
Was my beauty all in vain?
Advise me please, to end this pain!"

The mirror had been waiting patiently for her return, and this time it responded with an even more chilling direction:

"Your beauty, once beyond compare,
Soon will be no longer there.

Snow White is one like you once were.
Take and eat the heart of her!"

The queen whirled from the mirror in a rage and grabbed a nearby chair with the intention of hurling it at the offending mirror and shattering it once and for all. But she stopped short; partly because she believed the mirror offered her the only real hope, and partly because, in her undernourished state, she hadn't the strength to throw the chair. She sat down on the chair instead. She knew that she would indeed eat Snow White's heart if that was the only way to regain her beauty.

With this realization, the queen resolved to get it over quickly, and immediately sent for her most trusted servant to help her. This servant, however, was really a handsome prince disguising himself as the queen's servant in order to be closer to her, for he was secretly in love with her and waiting for the opportunity to win her heart.

The prince listened to the queen's request in shocked silence, staring at her with disbelief in his handsome blue eyes. Since true love was the only antidote to the sorcerer's evil spell, the prince had been completely unaware that the queen was nearing her expiration date. Indeed, in his eyes she was becoming more beautiful with each passing day.

But the prince could not refuse the queen anything, his love for her was so great, and so he readily agreed to help her. Recognizing this as the opportunity he had been waiting for, he added the condition that the queen spend that very evening with him, away from the castle. Desperate to have Snow White's heart, the queen agreed to the arrangement.

The prince found Snow White working in the kitchen, but the kind and gentle man had no intention of harming her. Instead, he took her deep into the woods to hide in safety; and then, coming upon a small lamb, he slaughtered it and carefully wrapped its heart. Content that he had done the right thing, he returned to the queen and presented the counterfeit heart to her.

The queen wasted no time in cooking the heart in low-calorie, non-saturated, high-omega oil and then tentatively took a bite of it. She could detect nothing unpleasant in the taste, but it nevertheless took every bit of her willpower to swallow it. The cruel spell that held her forced her onward until every last drop was consumed.

Afterward, the queen was anxious to stand before her mirror and see the results, but the prince firmly reminded her of her promise to go away with him, insisting that they leave immediately in order to reach their destination before nightfall. The prince's resolve won out and the two finally set out together.

They traveled deep into the woods, farther and farther away from the curse of the queen's land and into enchanted forests, until at last they came upon a small stone cottage that was nearly hidden by innumerable climbing vines of magically scented rosebushes. The overflowing branches ascended the stones and continued their advance until they were nearly covering the roof. As the couple approached, they breathed in the sweet fragrance that was drifting outward, engulfing them in its heady aroma. Whether it was the enchantment of those flowery vines that besieged it or the fact that it belonged to the prince, I know not, but neither the cottage nor its contents were touched by the sorcerer's spell.

The moment the queen walked through the small doorway and into the cottage, she felt overwhelmingly beautiful and cherished. The very walls seemed to embrace her, and she was filled with happiness. She thought this must be the effect of getting her youth back by eating Snow White's heart, but actually she was feeling the way she would have felt every day of her life, if only she had not been under the power of the wicked spell.

The queen turned to him with a radiant smile. He gazed at her and thought he had never seen her look so lovely. He took her hand and led her up a narrow stairway into a cozy sitting room. In the middle of the room, there stood a large mirror.

The prince gently placed the queen before the mirror. It was not enchanted, and so, for the first time in her life, the queen saw herself as she really was, and not by the warped standards maintained outside those cottage walls. She stared at herself in amazement.

The prince stood behind the queen and watched. He saw immediately that his plan had worked, and that the queen was finally seeing herself through his eyes. Then he saw her eyes meet his.

Suddenly, the queen's obsession with her own appearance disappeared, and she noticed how handsome her servant was. What an extraordinary couple they made as she gazed at the two of them in the mirror! She wondered how it was that she had never noticed how his thick, dark hair curled slightly at the ends. Or how his dark, smooth skin illuminated his intense blue eyes.

The prince watched the queen's face as she stared at him. His expectations for the evening had been minimal, namely, that the queen, within the safety of his forest, might realize the prince's feelings and accept his offer of courtship. He had not dared to hope for more than that, and was shocked to see the desire burning hotly in her eyes.

Perceiving her desire, he slowly began to undo the buttons

of her gown. She did not resist or tremble with fear that she would not be good enough, but instead shivered with anticipation. With a light swishing sound, the garment fell to the floor. She watched in silent wonder as his muscles strained under the control he applied to carefully remove her delicate clothing. She stood, as if hypnotized, while his large fingers painstakingly handled the sensitive fabric. For the first time in her life, she felt genuinely aroused.

One by one, her undergarments fell to the floor. She watched with interest as her body was slowly revealed. When she lifted her eyes to meet those of the prince in the mirror, the desire she saw there astonished her. With her heart throbbing within her breast, she met his gaze with the same burning intensity.

It was suddenly as if she were watching two strangers, so unfamiliar were the images in the mirror, and she could not pull her eyes away from the sight of them. She saw the woman shudder as her lover lowered his warm mouth to the back of her neck for a long, sensual kiss. He continued to kiss her lightly as his arms came around her waist and held her in a loving embrace. The woman's face was flushed, her lips were parted, and her breathing was quick.

The man in the mirror was steadily becoming more demanding as his hands began caressing the woman with a thoroughness that left no part of her untouched. This did not seem to offend her, however, for she only moaned softly as she stared intently ahead of her, wordlessly allowing him full access to her body. The queen watched with keen interest as the large, masculine hands roamed over every part of the woman. Her eyes followed every movement, every touch, every intimacy. A feeling of overpowering desire came over her as she watched.

Suddenly the man in the mirror pulled away from the

woman to remove his own clothing. Still, she continued to stare silently in front of her, as if she were under a spell. The queen wondered that she did not turn to watch her lover undress, so beautiful was his image, splendid in its arousal. He looked at his staring lady for a moment, and then turned toward the object of her interest. This made him smile, and he continued to look ahead with her, meeting the eyes of the queen, as he wrapped his arms around his lady and gently kissed the side of her face.

The queen felt herself tremble with anticipation as she watched the man now position himself behind the woman in the mirror. She parted her own legs slightly in imitation of the woman, as she watched her accommodate her lover. She imagined that she could feel his strong hands boring into her own hips as he held the woman firmly and pushed himself into her. It sounded like her own voice as the woman cried out with pleasure. The vision was so real that she fancied she could feel it when the man in the mirror penetrated his lady.

So completely wrapped up in the image before her was she that the queen did not even realize that she had begun to move her own hips in time with the woman she watched there. She marveled to see the intense expression of pleasure on that woman's face, the unrestrained moans escaping from her lips, and her hips undulating in such wild abandon.

Her own excitement increased as she watched every detail of the intimate performance that was being played out before her. She felt her upper body lean forward slightly as the man in the mirror gently encouraged his lover to do the same. His eyes met hers again in the mirror as he thrust himself into the woman, harder and faster.

Suddenly the queen was awakened from her spell and realized with a jolt that the woman in the mirror was no other than herself, and that it was her handsome servant who was staring back at her from his position behind her. She froze for a moment, suddenly embarrassed to have him see her thus.

Perceiving the change in his queen, the prince quickly turned her away from the mirror so that she was facing him. He kissed her tenderly and lifted her in his arms, carrying her to a nearby couch. But she glanced furtively back toward the mirror.

The prince held the queen close to him, joining himself with her again, all the while whispering soft endearments. The mirror seemed to give her assurance, and she strained her neck so that, always, she might watch the reflection in the mirror. And she watched herself do many extraordinary things throughout the night. The prince was delighted by her inquisitiveness, and was careful to make the long-awaited event last until she was completely satisfied.

Afterward, he continued to hold his queen close to him throughout the night, slowly caressing her body so that, by morning, not one single inch of her was left untouched or unloved. The queen smiled as she slept and dreamed of roses.

In the morning, the queen did not want to leave. But the prince knew that he must take her back to her castle, to see if his love had truly reached her heart and lifted her from the power of the curse.

The queen plucked one of the roses as she passed out through the doorway of the cottage and placed it in her bag, so that she might always remember the pleasure she found there. But as they traveled through the woods she became dispirited, and by the time they reached her castle she was overcome with anxiety. The prince reluctantly left her with a kiss and a promise to return later that day.

At her servant's departure, the queen lost no time in seeking her bedchamber mirror. Upon reaching it she gasped in horror. Nothing had changed since the last time she faced the horrid thing! She wasn't beautiful at all, but the same awful, expiring old woman she was the day before. Had the mirror lied and Snow White given up her life for naught?

The queen composed herself and addressed the mirror just so:

"Mirror, mirror, do not stall,
Or I shall tear you from that wall.
Tell me now, before I start,
What meant you, by Snow White's heart?"

She had less than a moment to wait before the mirror replied:

"Your lover is the fraud, I fear.
Snow White is safe, though far from here.
You must find her in the wood.
Through poison you may reach this good!"

Your lover is the fraud, I fear. So her servant had tricked her! The queen's eyes burned with unshed tears as she felt a cold rage creeping over her heart. The memory of the previous night in the cottage had been erased by the malevolent mirror and so, without another thought about it, the queen spent the remainder of the day creating a poison for Snow White. She carefully attached the poison to a beautifully carved, silver comb that, upon touching the head of Snow White, would immediately place her in a deep coma.

The prince noticed the change in the queen when he returned later that day. Her beautiful eyes flashed with anger as she relayed to him what the mirror had told her. He once again promised to help the queen by delivering the poisonous comb to Snow White, on the condition that she spend another night with him in his cottage.

But the good prince still had no intention of harming Snow White, and upon finding her in the woods, he asked for some of her hair, that he might attach it to the comb to temporarily appease his beloved queen. This Snow White readily agreed to, and the prince once again returned faulty evidence to his queen.

Upon seeing Snow White's hair upon the comb, the queen was filled with hope. She longed to stand before her mirror to see the results, but the prince insisted that she come straight-away with him, just as she had promised to do. She reluctantly agreed, and they arrived shortly thereafter at the cottage. And once again, upon entering the cottage, a feeling of joy and well-being came over the queen. She followed the prince this time to his bedchamber, where the wonderful little mirror now stood facing the bed.

Recollections of their activities on the previous night flashed through the queen's mind, and a wave of pleasure coursed through her at the memory. She undressed herself ex-citedly and lay on the prince's bed, facing the mirror, watching as the prince came up behind her and began stroking her body. She opened her legs. It delighted her to see her body in this position in the mirror, with the prince hovering over her, admiring and touching her. He caressed her backside leisurely, teasing her, until finally she arched her hips so that the open-ing between her legs touched his hand. He boldly delved into the wetness there, but the queen only gasped as she contin-ued to stare at her flushed face in the mirror.

Carefully, so as not to alarm her, the prince slowly lifted the queen's hips, adjusting her so that she was settled on her forearms and knees, with her hips at the highest point of elevation. She watched in utter astonishment, as the prince knelt behind her, staring intently at her most private place imaginable.

Without embarrassment or fear (for what had she now to fear when she felt so beautiful and so entirely cherished?), the queen watched her lover's excitement grow as he examined, pried, poked and kissed her intimate parts. She moaned with pleasure at the memory of what was to come. The prince seemed to read her thoughts, and he entered her from behind while she watched. The sight of him joining with her was almost as wonderful as the way it felt: his hardness sliding into her wet body, his large hands grasping her hips, his masculine features set in an expression of intense ecstasy.

She began to move, slowly at first, but then faster and faster, frantically rubbing herself against him, all the while delighting in the way her body appeared in the mirror, with her breasts jerking and bouncing and her buttocks shaking with every single thrust. It did not occur to her at all that the bouncing and shaking was unattractive, for the curse was far away from her mind. She dropped her head upon the bed as her body shuddered with bliss.

The next morning, the queen once again plucked one of the roses from its vine as she left the little cottage, and she began her journey home with a light heart. But old habits die hard and, no sooner had the latch clicked in the door upon the prince's departure, than the queen raced up to her bedchamber to learn what she would from the mirror. And a single glance in that glass caused the poor queen such anguish and disappointment that she collapsed on her bed in a heap, sobbing.

After she recovered from this outburst the queen faced the mirror once more, with the following words:

"Mirror, mirror, know I will—
Is my lover faithless still?
Did not the hairs upon the comb,
Prove Snow White is in her tomb?"

The mirror delayed not in responding:

"Snow White lives on, with beauty rare.
Her life could buy you years to spare.
You must weave her death of ilk
Into corset strings of silk!"

The queen was delighted with this new opportunity and immediately set to work, so that by the time the prince arrived at her doorstep later that afternoon she had the corset, with its deadly laces, ready and wrapped for her victim. But on this occasion the queen did not confide her true intentions to the prince. Instead, she convinced him that she had repented of her former behavior toward Snow White and wished him to deliver this present as way of an apology. The prince, completely unable to see any evil in his beloved queen, immediately took himself off to the woods to do as she bade him, after abstracting from her the promise to spend yet another evening in his cottage.

Snow White received the gift with great joy, and the prince, not suspecting any treachery from the queen, did not linger there but set forth immediately to make his return. As for Snow White, she could not resist the beautiful corset and nearly ripped her old clothes to shreds in her eagerness to try the elegant frippery on.

But no sooner had the corset touched her skin, than the stays, of their own accord, began to tighten, forcing a gasp from Snow White's lips and continuing until she was unable to take a single breath. She fell to the floor in a swoon and remained there, quite lifeless, until later that day, when she was discovered and placed in a beautiful glass coffin. But the remainder of Snow White's tale will have to wait until another time, for the prince is about to return to his queen, and I am certain that you would like to know what became of that poor lady.

To the prince's dismay, he returned to find the queen completely changed. Her skin seemed unnaturally taut, as if it had been stretched too tightly over her frame. Her eyes looked like those of a hawk, large and bulging. Her breasts were hard and unnatural looking and she was painfully thin. He realized instantly what she had done. But he loved her still and so, with less effort than it would take to pick up a small bird, he lifted the queen onto his horse and rode with her to his cottage.

But on this occasion, no roses were in bloom and the cottage seemed cheerless and damp. Upon entering the dwelling, the queen felt remorseful and wretched. She rushed up the stairs to the bedchamber in the hopes that the pleasure she had found there before would bring her comfort, but alas, upon peering into the unenchanted mirror, she gasped in horror. Her appearance was like something inhuman! She fell on the bed full of regret and weeping. She could not stay another minute in the cottage with the prince.

And so it was for three long months that the prince remained alone and unhappy, the queen remained a queen who was not expired, and Snow White remained in her glass coffin.

Then one day, while the queen was in her bedchamber,

she came upon the roses she had taken from the prince's cottage. To her amazement, they were completely intact and as fresh as the day she had picked them. She lifted them to her face, and their enchanted scent caused her to remember the time spent in the cottage with the prince. Suddenly she realized what she had given up and how unhappy she had been ever since. *I must undo this deed,* she thought.

With swift determination she grabbed the bed warmer from her bed and hurled it with all her might into the mirror, shattering it into a thousand pieces.

Next, she called for two messengers; the first of which she sent into the woods where Snow White slept in her coffin and the other she sent to her beloved servant. Then she waited.

The queen waited in her bedchamber for hours, but for her they passed like minutes. As the sun slowly made its way across the afternoon sky, she was thinking about her visits to the cottage, so charming with its countless vines of tiny, enchanted roses. Even when the light grew steadily dimmer through her window, her face glowed and flushed as she recalled the images in the bedroom mirror. When at last the shadows began to cast about for their evening positions, the queen's whole being ached for the soft and loving touch of her servant.

She fancied that she could feel a slight loosening of her flesh, and a sudden terror seized her; but she was awakened from her alarm by the sound of a footstep in the doorway and there, she beheld, her servant-prince!

Upon seeing the queen changed back to her former appearance, the prince nearly wept for joy. He calmed her fears by sweeping her into his arms and out through the doorway. They mounted his noble white horse, and that poor creature got no rest until he had carried the rapturous couple to the cottage deep in the wood.

And what they did there is exactly what you or I would be doing right now, if our own prince were here!

Mrs. Fox

It is to be expected that, at some point in any marriage, a wife might desire someone other than her husband. Such was the case with Mrs. Fox.

This is not to say that Mrs. Fox was discontent in her marriage with Mr. Fox, for the couple was exceedingly well matched. Mr. Fox was dashingly handsome and sophisticated, and Mrs. Fox was time and again captivated by his clever and amusing wit and charm. These glowing attributes of Mr. Fox perfectly complemented his wife's restless and inquisitive nature, which would have become discontented with a less-accomplished partner. What's more, Mr. Fox was gallantly attentive, and his romantic behavior only improved when met with Mrs. Fox's casual indifference, which made her seem quite mysterious to Mr. Fox. In short, their combined personalities produced a delightful give and take that they both enjoyed.

There was only one minute irregularity that arose in the Foxes' marriage; a pity that it was so inevitable. For beneath the detached exterior of Mrs. Fox lay an inquisitiveness that nearly drove her to distraction. When her curiosity was sufficiently piqued, she was apt to become impudently bold if she didn't check these tendencies behind a cool air of indifference. So, although she loved Mr. Fox above all things, these inclinations, when combined with her passionate temperament, brought about in her a tedium of things realized and a strong yearning for things new or forbidden.

Mr. Fox was unaware of any disturbance of this kind in his wife. He adored her passion for things unknown, and was thoroughly taken with her mysterious manner.

Now these yearnings of Mrs. Fox were not strange or foreign to her; they were, in fact, manifested in the form of one Mr. Wolfe.

Mr. Wolfe was Mr. Fox's dearest friend and fiercest rival. Since childhood, whenever any single thing had captured the attention of one, it immediately became a matter of supreme interest to the other, also. It was no different when Mr. Fox first noticed Mrs. Fox. Throughout their courtship Mr. Wolfe had been scandalously flirtatious, taking every opportunity to tempt and tease Mrs. Fox with brazen overtures. He was often slipping a moist tongue into a seemingly polite kiss on her hand, or leaving a steamy breath lingering salaciously in her ear behind an otherwise civil remark. While these little forbidden intimacies were unwanted and to all appearances ignored by Mrs. Fox, they always left her slightly atremble. Of course, once the Foxes were married, the rivalry had ended. Mr. Wolfe had accepted his defeat good-naturedly, and he even married soon thereafter, so that the matter was quite forgotten by everyone.

Everyone, that is, except Mrs. Fox.

Now Mrs. Wolfe was as simple and sweet as Mrs. Fox was passionate and complex. In truth, she was a much more suitable match for Mr. Wolfe's fiery, impulsive nature.

And Mrs. Fox certainly did not wish to be married to Mr. Wolfe, even if her thoughts did occasionally wander in the direction of the darker, more volatile man, sometimes even developing into wild speculations about how he performed his husbandly duties in the bedchamber. It did not signify anything lacking in her own marriage, for there was nothing amiss in her husband's treatment of her, and no single action of his with which she could find fault. On the contrary, Mr. Fox was as clever and skillful in the bedroom as he was in everything else. He knew exactly how to locate each and every nerve ending in Mrs. Fox's anatomy and, more important, what to do with them when he found them. He never took his own satisfaction before making quite sure of hers. To come to the point, Mr. Fox was everything Mrs. Fox could wish for in a lover.

Except, of course, that he was not Mr. Wolfe.

And aside from all of this, Mrs. Wolfe had come to be as dear a friend as Mrs. Fox could have. She genuinely enjoyed the company of sweet Mrs. Wolfe, in spite of the secret hunger for any little tidbit of information about the Wolfes' private life lurking within her. Mrs. Fox would simply compensate for this by boasting shamelessly about her own husband. She would go to great lengths to brag about the many admirable charms of Mr. Fox, all of which were absolutely true of course, but which nevertheless had lost some of their appeal simply because they were so readily available to her (unlike the forbidden charms of Mr. Wolfe). Mrs. Wolfe did not appear to notice this eccentricity in her friend, for she always seemed too absorbed by her own thoughts.

Time passed in this way, and you may think that Mrs. Fox's curiosity had diminished somewhat by frustration, but, no! It grew stronger. Poor Mrs. Fox could think of little else besides Mr. Wolfe and what it would be like to be Mrs. Wolfe. So preoccupied with these thoughts was Mrs. Fox that she could hardly enjoy the considerable physical talents of Mr. Fox without having her mind wander off into the Wolfes' boudoir. This is, in fact, what fueled her excitement as poor Mr. Fox spent his efforts pleasuring her. There was simply something so much more intriguing in the unknown and forbidden notion of Mr. Wolfe than in the familiar and real pleasures her husband had to offer. For Mrs. Fox, the grass was always greener somewhere else.

One day, as Mrs. Fox was guiltily prattling on about her husband's many capabilities to Mrs. Wolfe, the latter all of a sudden sighed miserably. "What a pity I cannot sample Mr. Fox's talents firsthand," she remarked absently.

No sooner were the words out of Mrs. Wolfe's mouth than the impact of what she had said hit her. She turned her eyes in horror to meet the shocked gaze of Mrs. Fox. Blushing a deep red, she was immediately contrite.

"Oh, my dear! I never meant...really...what I intended to say..." she stammered on, searching frantically for a way to recant the scandalous statement.

Mrs. Fox had at first been too dumbfounded to reply, such was her astonishment to hear those words uttered from the proper Mrs. Wolfe, but her composure quickly returned and she slyly took up the opportunity she had secretly wished for.

"It is, in truth, what I myself have wondered on occasion," she admitted. She did not dare to confess the extent of these wonderings, or that she had been thinking about little else since the wedding eve of the Wolfes' marriage.

"You…?" Sweet Mrs. Wolfe was still too flustered to contribute much to the conversation.

"It is only normal, after all," continued Mrs. Fox, determined to use her friend's unexpected slip to further her own wishes or, as it now stood, the wishes of them both.

"Our husbands, although each very talented I am sure, are in almost every respect opposites. How could we not wonder how it would feel to be with a man so different from our own?"

Mrs. Wolfe absorbed this and seemed to relax a bit.

"Perhaps," she consented. "But we could never…I mean," she stopped herself again.

"There is a way," suggested Mrs. Fox cunningly, with her heart pounding at her own boldness.

Mrs. Wolfe remained speechless, but there was a spark of interest in her eyes as they met Mrs. Fox's.

Mrs. Fox pretended to be contemplating the situation. In fact, she had played this scenario out in her mind at least a hundred times before.

"In a dark bedchamber," she mused, "our husbands would not be able to distinguish between us so easily."

Both women stared at the other in silence for a moment. Their hearts were racing at the implication of Mrs. Fox's words. Neither dared speak; then both spoke at once.

Mrs. Wolfe asked, "But, how?" Just as Mrs. Fox had wondered, "Would you really do it?"

The women couldn't suppress a nervous laugh. This released the tension a bit, and to Mrs. Fox's further amazement, Mrs. Wolfe spoke up first, in a breathless whisper, saying, "I would!"

Mrs. Fox could only marvel that Mrs. Wolfe was indeed full of surprises underneath that timid exterior!

The particulars were easily enough arranged once their intention had been established, and each woman eagerly did her part to prepare for the event. It seemed most logical that they simply change places during one of the many parties Mrs. Fox held, and where it was quite ordinary for the Wolfes and other guests to remain overnight. The other guests would add to the general confusion and hopefully diminish any idea of dissimilarity for their husbands.

As the date of the event drew near, both wives could not help going over and over their plans, not so much so that all would run smoothly as for the sheer thrill of reliving the excitement of what they were about to do, and to increase the anticipation of what was to come. Just imagining it caused both to become bright and rosy with expectation, and actually renewed their awareness of their own husbands in the meantime.

At last the night arrived when their long-awaited fantasy would be realized. The party itself was a long, tantalizing agony that left their nerves quaking.

After the party Mrs. Fox shivered in anticipation as she lay beside her husband and waited for him to fall asleep. His arms tightened around her protectively in response. She wondered how Mrs. Wolfe was faring. They had both agreed to gently put off any advances from their husbands. Later, the impostor wives would have a change of heart. There was no doubt that both husbands would accommodate their belated "wives"; they were, after all, men, no matter how different from one another, and it would be a singular thing indeed if one of them were to fail on this night.

Mrs. Fox listened keenly as her husband's breathing slowed and his arms around her relaxed. At last he was asleep! She cautiously slipped from the bed without disturbing him and tiptoed out of their chamber.

Mrs. Wolfe was already waiting for her in the shadows of the hallway. The conspirators exchanged a quick hug and then scurried away into their new chambers.

Mrs. Fox did not think of what Mrs. Wolfe was about to do with her own husband, for she was too overcome with excitement over what was about to happen to herself. Besides, whatever they did together, her husband would think it was no other than she he was doing it with.

With her heart hammering wildly within her breast she tiptoed into the pitch-dark chamber where Mr. Wolfe slept, slipped off her nightgown and crept into the bed beside him. He groaned in his sleep as she rubbed her naked body against his. His hands instinctively went around her and pulled her closer to him.

Mrs. Fox lifted her face and found Mr. Wolfe's warm, moist lips. The stubble on his cheek was rougher than that of her husband's. He responded immediately to her kiss, even in sleep, and his arms tightened around her as he all but bruised her lips with his. All at once he was awake.

Mr. Wolfe did not question or tease, as her husband might have done, but instead he reacted violently, flinging her onto her back and covering her body with his own. Although she was alarmed by his brutality, there was no opportunity for second thoughts, for he held her down securely and crushed her lips under his. But she was having no second thoughts, or, if she had, they were almost immediately forgotten in the tumult of his embrace.

Her hands had flown up in a gesture at first defensive, but so ineffectual as a defense that they really seemed more of a caress. She spread out her hands over his chest and fingered the curly hair that covered his burly muscles, so different from her husband's smooth, lean body. Longing to feel his roughness fully against her skin, she wrapped her arms around his neck and arched her back, pressing her bare breasts against him. His body was so warm and hard and strong. She shuddered.

"I'm sorry, my love," he murmured. "I know I frighten you when I am too rough." He began to loosen his hold on her.

"No!" she protested. Then, collecting herself, she whispered to disguise her voice. "I want it like that, darling."

There was silence for a moment, and Mrs. Fox wondered if she had given herself away.

"Are you sure?" he asked her at last.

"Yes," she whispered. "Hold nothing back from me tonight."

He moaned out loud and then lowered his lips to hers, pausing directly over her lips, nearly but not quite touching, for a brief moment. She could feel his hot breath on her face as he once again murmured, "You're sure?"

"Yes! Yes!" she whispered. "Plea…" But she could not finish her petition because his lips were once again crushing hers.

Mr. Wolfe pushed his tongue into Mrs. Fox's mouth, tasting her lips and tongue. Next he was kissing her cheeks, chin and neck. Everywhere he kissed her he seared her skin with his hot breath and rough face. Her flesh burned and tingled from his lips and tongue. He licked and bit her breasts, making her cry out. Then he moved over her belly and lower, covering every inch of her with his kisses. Spreading her legs wide, he buried his tongue deep within her. He was like a ravenous animal; his mouth seemed to be everywhere at once. But he still did not satisfy, no! His tongue continued to seek out every part of her so that, before he had finished, he had tasted every hidden place between her wide-open legs. And even though the room was pitch-dark, Mrs. Fox's cheeks burned red-hot with embarrassment. But she could not wiggle away from him; he held her much too firmly for that! His lips and tongue took possession of her, greedily, and without the slightest regard for her self-conscious struggles.

At last Mr. Wolfe withdrew his tongue, but alas, she had overcome her embarrassment and now ached for him to continue! He had other plans however and, placing her knees so that one rested on each of his shoulders, he drew himself nearer to her again, stretching her legs awkwardly up and apart as he did so. Holding her securely so that she would not move away, he pressed himself into her. She cried out loudly when she felt how large he was. All her control seemed to be draining away and she cried out again and again as he began to drive into her. And as her excitement grew he increased his speed.

Although Mrs. Fox loved being thus laid open and taken, she lamented that she could not move at all in her present position.

As if reading her mind, Mr. Wolfe suddenly flipped her onto her stomach, and pulled her up onto her knees. Mrs. Fox succumbed without delay, and gasped when he reentered her from behind. He reached around her body and vigorously pinched the tips of her breasts with his strong fingers, while steadily working himself into her. She gasped with outrage and mortified delight.

He was steadily becoming more crude and demanding. His impostor wife unconsciously edged forward a little to escape his hard thrusts, but he grabbed a handful of her hair and yanked, forcing her body back and obliging her to stay put unless she wished to suffer further pain. She cried out again, but he seemed not to hear her. If anything, he was becoming even more ruthless with each of her cries. She thrashed about desperately, trying to lessen the blow of each punishing thrust, but again, her attempts only incited him further. Tears streamed down her face as she was obliged to remain still and withstand the relentless onslaught. She hated Mr. Wolfe; though an irrepressible yearning possessed her in spite of her discomfort and anger. She wondered how Mrs. Wolfe was able to withstand this rough mating, even as she was reaching between her legs to enhance her own pleasure.

She was slowly becoming conscious of her other senses, and particularly she was aware of a sound that had been echoing in her eardrums. It was a foreign sound, low and base and harsh; mere whispers and grunts but with the tone and inflection of longing and horror and shame. The disquieting sound had been echoing in her ears for some time now. But what was it?

Suddenly she was filled with revulsion. It was her! It was the sound of her own voice, half whispering and half grunting out her surreptitious wish, again and again.

"Harder," she heard herself moan. "Harder, harder, I want it harder!"

How long had she been repeating that shameful directive through her struggles and tears? How much more could she take? Yet even fully conscious of it she couldn't seem to stop; she just kept choking out the words "Harder…I want it harder."

Mrs. Fox felt like a woman possessed. Her desire was controlling and overpowering her. Her initial horror over what she was doing had halted her sensations for but a moment, then they returned with twice the strength. She didn't know what to do. She was terrified that it would end before she had had enough.

"Please, oh, please," she was begging and sobbing now,

"don't stop! You mustn't stop." Through her sobs she continued to pleasure herself, even as her poor aching body flinched and cowered from his fierce riding of her. And she realized that this was how she knew it would be with Mr. Wolfe. She could hardly account for her desire for him, but she still wanted more!

She clung to the bed in an attempt to hold her ground against his pounding, and she knew now that it was she who egged him on with her frenzied mantra "Harder, harder." She wished she could stop herself. This was madness. But even so, her trembling fingers kept rubbing and rubbing and her lips kept repeating, "Harder, harder, harder!"

Mr. Wolfe grabbed hold of Mrs. Fox by her buttocks, and he squeezed each one brutally. Then he dug his fingers in and used them to pile drive himself deeper into her still, asking, "Is that hard enough?"

Insane lust was dominating Mrs. Fox, so that even though she sobbed in agony she still kept whimpering, "Harder… harder!"

Mr. Wolfe was now working her hips like kneaded bread, his large fingers digging into her fleshy buttocks and manipulating her tender cheeks in and around his shaft. Her head had collapsed onto the bed but he still held her buttocks quite high, squeezing and pinching as he simultaneously pulled her toward him and thrust into her. He too was becoming quite crazed from her maddening chant, begging him to go harder, faster, and above all, not to stop. Her bottom had become like dough in his fists as he continued to pound himself into her softness.

Mrs. Fox at last reached the height of her excitement. She squeezed her eyes shut as the waves came over her, her body nearly broken but her lips still murmuring over and over,

"Harder, harder, harder." Her entire being convulsed in shudders of unspeakable pleasure.

Feeling her shudders and hearing her soft cries, Mr. Wolfe lost all control. Mrs. Fox felt his body quake, as with a loud yell he flung himself deep within her one last time.

When it was over he took her in his arms. She was trembling violently and he suddenly became very gentle, begging her forgiveness for his rough treatment of her. He spread tender kisses over her face and shoulders, cursing himself and pleading with her to forgive him. Finally her trembling lessened and only then did he fall into deep slumber. With her face still damp from her tears, Mrs. Fox crept from the bed and left the Wolfes' chamber with a fervent wish to be with her own gentle husband.

Meanwhile, you mustn't think that Mrs. Wolfe had been sluggish in waking Mr. Fox, for she had sneaked her way into his arms much the same as Mrs. Fox had done.

"What's this now?" Mr. Fox teased when he felt her silky softness snuggling up against him.

But there was no need for Mrs. Wolfe to answer, for his lips were claiming hers in a gentle teasing kiss. Excitement filled her as she wound her arms around his neck. His skin was so warm and lean and smooth she could not help herself from pressing her nakedness up tightly against him. He kissed her masterfully, nipping at her lips and teasing her with his tongue.

As Mr. Fox kissed Mrs. Wolfe, his hands gently wandered down the length of her body, caressing and lightly tickling her skin to create goose bumps and cause her breasts to harden. Then his hands moved to her breasts that he might enjoy his handiwork. His fingertips determinedly squeezed and twisted the hard little tips. Mrs. Wolfe gasped at this exquisitely sweet torture. Mrs. Fox certainly had not lied when she described how talented her husband was.

Mr. Fox took his time, not greedily grabbing and grasping, but playfully handling her breasts until she thought she might die from the agony of not being touched elsewhere. At last, just as she thought she might lose her mind, he finally moved his hand lower, but then he lingered on her belly, until she lifted her hips off the bed and pushed them upward and into his hand. Mr. Fox laughed at her obvious impatience, and whispered, "Easy, love."

Mrs. Wolfe had never been in the position of having to wait or plead; in fact she was quite used to being attended to without delay. This teasing created a twisting ache between her legs and a prickling awareness in her nerve endings, so she felt all at once needy and desperate and irritable. She lifted her hips and pushed them fiercely into his hand yet again, silently cursing him for his cool control. Chuckling at her obvious displeasure in him, he kept circling her skin with cruel gentleness, lightly brushing around and between her wide-open legs but all too quickly flittering away again to roam over her hips, belly and thighs, and then back between her legs.

Mrs. Wolfe was becoming quite anxious but what could she do? Fearing to say the wrong thing and give herself away she could do no more than wait. However, her need was becoming voracious and the little flickering teasing touches, although quite expert in effectiveness, were all too short-lived to even come close to satisfying her. She moaned in anguish and shamelessly flung her hips up again in search of his hand. She was becoming more and more indignant with Mr. Fox. How did Mrs. Fox bear all this horrible teasing?

Mr. Fox, meanwhile, seemed to be enjoying himself too much to care about her discomfort. He merely laughed at her struggles, using his hands to subdue her even as they drove her to distraction. He loved how each time he brushed and teased the opening between her legs it seemed to get wetter and wetter. He staunchly approved discipline and self-control, and furthermore believed that for every moan of anticipation one full second of pleasure was added to the final satisfaction. He kept this in mind as his fingers continued their torturous dance over her body. His own body was throbbing with eagerness to bury itself in her wetness and get lost in the pleasure. But all in good time.

Besides that, Mr. Fox loved touching his wife. It seemed that every time he did she felt new and exciting. He especially enjoyed finding her most sensitive places, and once she was properly warmed, she was that much more likely to submit to these more inquisitive ministrations. Feeling that she was in such a condition as that now, his hands slowly worked their way up her thighs, spreading them even farther apart. He kissed her between her legs while slipping one hand up below. His tongue slowly trailed the soaking slit to her opening as his finger snaked its way up between her two plump buttocks and rested at the puckered hole there. Mrs. Wolfe was too stunned to move, so her legs remained wide-open, and her fingers grasped the bedsheets at her sides. Every molecule was screaming in mutiny, yet waiting obediently for release. She, in turns, gasped and moaned.

Mr. Fox was meanwhile leisurely circling her backside with his finger while simultaneously tickling her pleasure spot knowingly with his tongue. He did this with an almost uncanny expertise, flicking his tongue over the sensitive area with just the right amount of force and pressure to send thrills throughout her body, and then stopping abruptly to lap up her liquids with a wicked laugh. Meanwhile, his finger between her buttocks continued its teasing and circling, even pushing into her now and then, farther and farther, encouraged by her little gasps.

Mrs. Wolfe reflected that, as forceful as her husband was, she had never before felt so utterly abused. While Mr. Wolfe took what he wanted from her she was able to take what she wanted from him, too. But this was different somehow. It felt as if Mr. Fox was controlling them both; and she did not like it one bit. Tears came to her eyes and she cried out in frustration and impatience.

Now Mr. Fox reckoned he at last had her where he wanted her. He laid back on the bed, saying, "Come now and get it."

Mrs. Wolfe was stunned. She had certainly never heard such an utterance from Mr. Wolfe. She had never seen a man show such control.

But she could not keep herself from continuing, for she sorely needed what he was withholding. So up she got, and prepared to mount Mr. Fox.

However, this was not exactly what Mr. Fox had intended. He stopped her before he entered her.

"First show me how much you want it."

Oh, how she hated him! She almost forgot herself in the heat of her anger, and told him what she thought of him. Seemingly unaware of this, his hand was gently caressing her head and stroking her hair, even as he pressed her head downward. She choked back her indignation and opened her mouth to accept his hard shaft. He kept pressing her head down until she could feel him at the back of her throat.

"That's it," he groaned with pleasure. "If you want it you're going to have to work for it."

Her face burned when she heard these words, but the distress between her legs was becoming urgent, so what could she do?

Mrs. Wolfe worked with all her might to please Mr. Fox, licking and sucking as cleverly as she was capable and even using her hands too, just as he had done, so that she might earn her reward. She sucked and slurped until she was certain she had never done it so well, and she even thought up some new things that she hadn't thought of before; such was her desire to win the pleasures Mr. Fox dangled before her. And it occurred to her that this, too, was causing her loins to ache even more painfully than Mr. Fox's clever administrations had.

But, oh, how much longer until she would be granted relief? Tears filled her eyes as she continued to labor before him, nearly choking herself in her efforts to please him.

Mr. Fox was a firm believer in self-control as we have established, but he was not a machine, and his body also had its limitations. He abruptly stopped the suckling therefore, lest he should shame himself and disappoint his partner after all her commendable efforts. He said, "You have well earned your reward!" And he pulled her onto his throbbing body.

Mrs. Wolfe moaned loudly as her body was lowered onto his. It felt so good to finally have him sliding into her! At last the ache between her legs started to recede a bit as she wiggled herself up and down and forward and back, trying to get the feeling just right.

Mr. Fox was fondling and pinching her breasts, but as Mrs. Wolfe's movements became more frenzied he moved one hand down between her legs and began to help her. She gasped and moaned, once again amazed by how clever Mr. Fox was. His fingers were much more effective than her rubbing had been and she slowed her own movements to a mere rocking motion and allowed his talented fingers to do the rest. She rocked and ground her hips forward and back as his fingers twisted and teased. With his other hand he pinched the tips of her breasts.

Mrs. Wolfe was unused to this gentler style of intercourse. Her husband's more vigorous attentions revealed to her his attraction and need. Mr. Fox's absolute composure seemed almost like indifference by comparison, even if it did enhance the pleasure considerably. She closed her eyes and imagined her husband ravishing poor Mrs. Fox and this brought about a most shattering conclusion to her painstaking efforts of the evening.

She collapsed onto Mr. Fox. He wrapped his arms around her, holding her firmly by the shoulders as he repeatedly thrust himself into her. She clung to him, trembling as he released himself into her. And Mrs. Wolfe forgot everything for a while, simply luxuriating in the soft afterglow of their lovemaking. But at last she perceived that Mr. Fox had fallen asleep, with her still rested atop and astride him. She silently extricated herself from his embrace, careful not to wake him. Then she quickly dressed and left the Foxes' bedroom.

Mrs. Fox was there to meet her in the dim hallway, and their eyes met and examined the other for a brief moment in silence. Mrs. Wolfe blushed as she wondered what Mrs. Fox must think after having this firsthand knowledge of her husband. But Mrs. Fox was experiencing the same embarrassment as she wondered the same thing! And both realized that they were better suited to their own husbands after all.

Perhaps the reader now expects me to reiterate the sage adage that the grass isn't greener on the other side, and that people ought to be content with what they have. But I'm not sure that would be the appropriate conclusion to draw from this particular tale, for Mrs. Fox and Mrs. Wolfe continue their occasional excursions into the other's bedrooms to this very day. And while it is quite true that the grass was not actually greener on the other side for either one, it turns out that it was still fairly green, after all.

And there really are so many shades of green anyway, aren't there?

Snow White
in the Woods

Once upon a time there lived a king and queen who had everything they wanted—except a child. On cold winter evenings they would sit contentedly near the cozy hearth, the queen with her needlepoint and the king watching her, while both discussed the day's events. But every now and then, the queen would halt all activity to stare out the window at the falling snow, and there she would gaze, having completely forgotten her unfinished sentence or her needle suspended in midair. Her husband knew well what it was that arrested her attention on these occasions; she was envisioning their child.

On one such evening, the queen accidentally pricked her finger with her sewing needle. A bright red drop of blood appeared and, as the queen stared at it, she sighed deeply and murmured, "If only I could have a daughter with lips as red as this blood, skin as white as the snow outside and hair as black as the coal that burns in the fire!"

Within a year the queen's wish came to pass, and the happy couple were blessed with a daughter who had lips as red as blood, skin as white as snow and hair as black as coal. They called her Snow White.

The queen died shortly after the birth of her daughter, and a few years later her husband remarried. His new wife made a beautiful queen, and the three lived together happily for a time. But before Snow White was ten years of age her father died also, leaving her to be raised by her stepmother. The woman was kind to the child at first, but with each year that passed Snow White became more and more beautiful and, by degrees, her stepmother, who was aging and fearful of losing her own beauty, began to resent her. One day, the queen abruptly stopped the supply of beautiful gowns and other adornments that Snow White was accustomed to, and forced her to labor in the kitchen. But even in rags, Snow White's beauty could not be ignored, and to her stepmother, who was plagued day and night by the fear of losing her beauty, it seemed as if Snow White were growing more beautiful for the sole purpose of tormenting her.

Finally the queen could endure Snow White's presence no longer, so she had a servant take her away with instructions to put her to death. But the gentle servant did not harm Snow White. Instead, he took her far away into the woods and warned her of the queen's intentions. Snow White was terrified, but the servant assured her that only a short distance farther she would find a small cottage belonging to seven kind little men who lived together in the wood. The dwarfs, he promised, would keep her safe.

When the servant left her, Snow White was alone for the first time in her life. The woods were filled with strange noises, and she rushed about in search of the dwarfs' cottage. She wound her way deeper and deeper into the woods until, at length, she reached a small bungalow that could be none other than the home of the dwarfs, for the doorway was so short as to oblige Snow White to bend in order to enter through it.

With curiosity now overriding her fears, Snow White knocked several times on the small door. Realizing the dwarfs must be out, and impatient to see inside the little hut, she opened the door and let herself in.

Once inside, there remained no doubt that this was indeed the cottage of the dwarfs, for there were seven little chairs around the kitchen table, and seven place settings upon the table, and so forth. As Snow White advanced farther into the cottage, she beheld seven little chairs in a quaint little sitting room and, farther on, seven neatly made little beds in the bedroom. *What sort of men are these?* she wondered.

Now, the seven dwarfs were really seven handsome princes who had been placed under an evil spell by an angry witch. The spell, in addition to making the princes very small in stature, also caused each of them to be afflicted with a malady of sorts, so that one was plagued by continuous fits of sneezing, another by chronic sleepiness, another still by a sour disposition, and so on. Seeing no relief from their wretched situation, the princes left polite society to live quietly together in the woods, where eventually they came to be known by the characteristics they were given from the curse, so that they were called Sneezy, Sleepy, Grumpy, Happy, Dopey, Bashful and Doc. Such were the circumstances of the dwarfs when they made the acquaintance of Snow White later that evening.

From their very first meeting, Snow White was charmed by the dwarfs and felt quite safe residing with them in their little bungalow in the woods. And as for the prince-dwarfs, they each fell deeply in love with Snow White. Nothing she did failed to please them, and they doted on her in every single thing that she wished. In no time at all they became the best of friends.

Now it happened one evening that the prince-dwarfs overheard Snow White crying in her bed. Alarmed, they rushed to her side and begged her to tell them the cause of her distress. After much prodding, Snow White finally confessed her loneliness to the dwarfs, and told them of her deepest desire for a prince of her own to love. This declaration saddened the dwarfs greatly; but Doc suddenly announced that he knew a remedy for Snow White.

"What is it?" she asked.

Doc did not answer her question, asking her instead, "Do you trust your devoted dwarfs, Snow White?"

"Of course!" she cried.

"Lie down and close your eyes, then, and we shall see," he continued.

Snow White complied, and at length she felt the hands of all seven of the little men upon her body, lifting her nightdress and alighting on her bare skin.

Snow White gasped and jumped up from the bed. Whatever she had expected, it was certainly not that!

"Things are not always as they appear, dearest Snow White," advised Doc. "But we can do little to help until you are able to trust us."

And with that he and his six companions left Snow White alone with her misery.

The incident was quickly forgotten, and once again the friendship between the eight blossomed. But Snow White was still plagued in the evenings with an aching loneliness, and one night her sobs were once again heard by the dwarfs.

They rushed to Snow White's side with inquiries and entreaties. She again explained her melancholy wish for a prince of her own to love. And once again, Doc made the claim that he knew a cure.

"Please, tell me!" cried Snow White.

"Do you trust your faithful dwarfs?" he asked her.

"Yes!" she swore.

"Then lie back and close your eyes," he instructed.

Snow White did this, and within seconds she once again felt the small hands of all seven men upon her body. She gasped and jumped up. *What on earth could they be thinking?* she wondered.

"Be calm, for we could never harm you, Snow White," Doc quieted her, adding sadly, "it is enough that you still do not trust us."

And with that the seven little men left her quite alone.

The matter was again forgotten and, as the months passed and the cool winds brought snow into the forest, Snow White and the seven dwarfs grew closer than ever in the cozy little cottage. And yet, poor Snow White lamented the absence of a prince of her own to love, for all princesses cannot help but yearn for a prince. And soon the dwarfs were once again troubled by the sound of her tears.

They immediately rushed to her side, much as they had done before. She told them yet again of her desire for a princely lover. And again Doc swore he knew a cure for her loneliness.

"Do you trust your loyal dwarfs?" he asked her, just as he had before.

"With all my heart!" Snow White cried.

"Then lie back and close your eyes," said he.

This she did, and just like before she felt the light touches of the dwarfs hands, as soft as mere breaths, descending upon her face and body. She did not jump up this time, but trusted that they would not bring her to any harm.

Snow White willed her body to relax and, as she did so, warmth crept steadily over her, enveloping her in heat, and a strange tingling sensation began to stir up from within her. The fingers soon gave way to soft, moist lips that sought hers. At the first kiss to touch her lips Snow White opened her eyes, and standing before her she beheld the most beautiful prince she had ever seen. He held her hand while a second kiss claimed her lips and, there, before her gaping eyes, appeared an even more handsome prince, and then another, and still another, until the seven dwarfs had all regained their princely form, each more magnificent than the last. Every prince was uniquely different from the others, yet all of them were striking in their masculinity and physical perfection. One had flaxen hair and eyes of blue, while another had russet colored hair and dark eyes. One chest was covered in manly curls, while another remained as smooth as silk. Even the color of their skin was singular and unique amid them, for the flesh of one prince was as black as coal, while another's was the color of stained walnut, and still another had skin that was exceedingly fair. In short, there was not one masculine characteristic, no matter how minute, lacking among the seven men.

Snow White was positively trembling with shock and delight. "Choose your prince," she heard one of them whisper close to her ear. But she remained silent, for she could not bear the thought of losing so much as one of the magnificent princes that stood before her.

The princes did not question her silence. Instead, they knowingly removed their clothes, which had been all but torn to shreds in their transformation. Next, they set out to remove Snow White's nightdress, and it quickly disappeared as a flurry of fourteen agile hands set to action. Relieved of the impediment of her gown, the hands were now free to caress her flushed, trembling body thoroughly, seeking out every curve and dimple and peak, and finding all her hidden places. The hands explored her fully, lingering here and there, but leaving no single part of her untouched. Meanwhile their lips devoured hers in turn.

But the hungry mouths grew too impatient to wait idly for a turn at Snow White's lips, so they sought out other places to kiss. Feverishly Snow White moaned and writhed as the hands and lips of the seven princes consumed every part of her. She shivered as she felt the sharp teeth of one prince nip carefully at her breast, while another prince gently suckled at the other. One tongue slid down the length of her belly as another wriggled its way into her body at the juncture between her legs. Another set of lips took hers in a deep and lingering kiss.

Snow White was so overcome with excitement and desire that it was a struggle to keep breathing, and for a moment she feared she might lose consciousness. She floundered near delirium as she anxiously waited for what would come next.

Perceiving her quandary and the remedy for it, the princes gently positioned Snow White's body so that she could receive her first prince, a beautiful man with golden hair and eyes of the deepest blue. He kissed her tenderly as he slowly came into her. Snow White cried out in irrepressible ecstasy, utterly beside herself with the pleasure she felt.

You mustn't think that the other princes remained idle in

the meantime. One prince held up her right leg while another prince held up her left. A third prince kissed her lips while two more kissed and licked her breasts. They all watched the fair prince take Snow White, patiently waiting for their own turn, and she had to close her eyes for a moment just to catch her breath.

Just as Snow White was approaching the height of her pleasure with the gentle blond prince, the men who held her legs opened them wider and higher so that the prince could thrust himself deeper within her. This maneuver quickly had its effect, and all eyes watched the pair as they submitted to the last rushes of pleasure.

Immediately afterward, the fair prince stepped aside and another, darker prince took his place. This prince was not as gentle as the first, but he pleased Snow White just as much, if not more. With his eyes staring fiercely into hers, he twisted her body at the waist, so that her left leg crossed over to the far right. With the aid of the other princes, who held her in the desired position, the dark prince took Snow White while never once letting his eyes leave hers. Once again, her excitement and desire began churning and growing within her. With so many princes to attend to her, there was nothing more for her to do—indeed, there was nothing more she *could* do—than to simply lie there and accept the pleasure offered her by their combined efforts. And that is just what Snow White did. She was keenly aware of the individual princes as they administered to her, and acutely conscious of each and every touch of their fingers and lips. The princes held her firmly, while her dark lover thrust himself repeatedly into her, enjoying her, yet careful not to shame himself by putting his own pleasure before hers. Snow White strained and moaned as the sweet agony continued to build inside her, until she once again shuddered in fulfillment, together with her dark prince.

Moments later the dark prince was replaced by yet another dashing princely lover. His eyes were a deep emerald green, and his handsome smile displayed perfect, white teeth. With Snow White still in the position she had been left in by the other prince, with one leg crossing over to the side, the green-eyed prince pressed into her, kissing her lips tenderly as he did so. In the next instant her skillful lover eased her over and onto her knees, without the slightest discomfort to her, and after which she was still joined to him!

Snow White stared out blindly in front of her as the prince took her with slow, long thrusts from behind. The other princes, meanwhile, continued to touch her, with intimate caresses along her buttocks and thighs, probing and prodding, as they each eagerly anticipated their own turn to stand between those soft legs and fill the opening within.

Snow White looked up and beheld the black-skinned prince standing near her. Positioned as she was, her head reached the precise height of his hips, which were so close that his manhood, rigid and throbbing, was poised directly in front of her within inches of her lips. He stroked her shoulders and back gently as he watched the other prince thrust himself into her.

Snow White stared at the dark protrusion in wonder. Her mouth was opened slightly from the little gasps and shrieks that escaped through her lips, and now, she perceived that her black prince was edging forward slowly, ever so slowly, until finally his wetness could be felt upon her lips. He did not force himself into her mouth, however, but waited for her lips to open wider, which they did of their own accord, and in the next instant he was fully inside her. Tremendously aroused yet again, she rocked her body back and forth, delighting in the abandon. How she had longed for a single prince to pleasure her. Now she would never be content with only one!

And so the princes served Snow White worthily, each in a different and unique way, until she had sampled the gifts of all seven. And even when it was not their turn to please her, they continued to minister to her faithfully, assisting her in every way they could devise for her to achieve the maximum amount of pleasure. At last exhausted, she drifted off into a very deep sleep.

The next morning Snow White woke up alone and almost fancied that she had dreamed the entire episode, except that throughout her body she felt tiny evidences that she had indeed been ravished the night before. *But where have my princes gone to?* she wondered. And where had they come from? She was left to ponder this for the remainder of the day, until at last the seven dwarfs came home that evening. But seeing them, Snow White felt quite shy, and wondered how she should approach the subject.

Snow White remained silent through dinner, but memories of the previous night flashed in and out of her mind. Feverishly she fought off the images, but they continued to assail her until she cried, "Where are my princes?"

Within seconds the dwarfs' true identities were explained to her. Snow White had only to kiss the lips of any dwarf of her choosing to free him, if only temporarily, from the evil spell. How Snow White rejoiced to hear this! And yet, she once again wondered how she would be able to choose one over the other. In examining each of their faces, she could clearly see that they were all equally devoted to her.

"I cannot choose between you, my dearest princes," she said to the dwarfs. "How could I?"

The dwarfs glanced at each other. They had never denied her anything she wished, and they could not do so now.

"You may see all your princes again if that is what you wish, Snow White," Doc told her kindly. "It is entirely up to you."

Snow White approached Doc then and, closing her eyes, gently kissed his lips. She opened her eyes to see her beautiful blond gentle prince standing before her. Then she went to where Grumpy stood and kissed his lips. There stood her dark, rougher prince. A tingle went through her as she kissed one dwarf after another and discovered their true identities. She led the princes to the bedroom and allowed them to slowly remove her clothing. She was shaking with desire as she stood naked before her seven princely lovers. She moved into the circle of princes and allowed herself to be drowned in pleasure.

Night after night Snow White spent with the seven princes, and time passed quickly by. Now and then word would come to her from the castle of the queen, but this did not concern Snow White, for she was convinced that the dwarfs would keep all harm from her.

One day, a servant came to deliver a message from the queen, who now claimed to have much remorse and distress over the past injustices done to Snow White. The servant presented Snow White with a gift from the queen, to prove her change of heart. But this servant had been fooled by the queen, for she still wished for Snow White's death.

Snow White accepted the gift with misgivings. She did not question the dubious nature of the queen's offering, as she should have, but rather, was frightened by the prospect of leaving her handsome princes, should the queen demand that Snow White return to the castle.

Thoughtfully, Snow White opened the queen's gift. She started with delight when she saw the beautiful silk corset within. Thinking only of her princes and how they would react when they beheld her in the exotic little frippery, she rushed to try it on. But the moment it touched her skin, the corset, which was cursed by an evil spell, suddenly began to close in around her body, tightening of its own accord until Snow White could no longer draw a single breath. She fell to the floor in a swoon, and remained there, still as death.

When the seven dwarfs returned to the cottage later that day, they found Snow White where she had fallen, seemingly dead. Overcome with grief, the dwarfs laid Snow White upon one of the beds, and then set out to build her a beautiful coffin of carved mahogany. The coffin took many days to finish, but at last, when the time came to bury her, she still looked so beautiful and full of life that none of them could bear to close the lid. They made her another coffin of glass, and into this they placed Snow White. Every day without fail the dwarfs visited her to pay homage, gazing upon her rapturously and grieving miserably for their untimely loss.

Several months passed until, one day, the queen truly did repent of her unkindness to Snow White. She sent another servant into the woods with instructions to cut the stays of Snow White's corset and set her free from the evil spell.

But this servant was unfamiliar with the forest and the cottage of the dwarfs and, after much meandering in and around the area, he became lost. Afraid to return to the queen without accomplishing his mission, he sat down under a tree to contemplate the matter. By and by, a handsome prince rode through on his white horse.

The servant flagged down the prince to beg his assistance in the errand of the queen and, as princes are known to ride through forests for opportunities just like this, the prince enthusiastically agreed to find and save the fair Snow White.

The handsome prince easily found the cottage of the dwarfs and within minutes discovered Snow White in her glass coffin. He lifted the cover and stared at her for a moment before reaching beneath her and breaking apart her stays. She immediately awoke, and stared at the handsome prince.

"I love you, Snow White," he said. "Marry me and be my princess."

Now Snow White was forever forgetting which dwarf became which prince, but she knew without a doubt that this prince was not one of hers. "I cannot marry you," she replied, looking around for her own princes.

The prince was shocked; he had been so certain that that was not how the story went, but, after much ado, he finally gave up and left Snow White at the cottage of the dwarfs. And, oh, what celebrating took place there when the dwarf-princes returned to discover Snow White alive and well!

The queen, of course, made repeated attempts to bring Snow White back to the castle but, to everyone's astonishment, Snow White adamantly refused. Every manner of enticement and coercion was employed, but nothing could persuade Snow White to return. Eventually, the queen was forced to relent, and Snow White was permitted to remain in the little cottage with the dwarfs.

The strange behavior of Snow White caused many a rumor to spring up, but the queen and those in her service most tirelessly maintain that Snow White did, in fact, marry the prince who saved her in the woods, riding off with him to his kingdom far away. Perhaps that is even the story that you heard.

But I can assure you that Snow White stayed in the little cottage of the dwarfs, hidden deep in the forest. No doubt she is still there today.

The Empress' New Clothes

This is a story about an empress. During the mystical era of her reign, there were many empresses and queens in power throughout the world. It is said that these legendary women ruled judiciously, and that they brought about a most remarkable amity between their kingdoms and the nations that surrounded them. And as for their subjects, well, you've never heard a single instance of revolt, have you? Indeed not, for these women were supreme leaders, and one of the greatest mysteries in history is that they lost their power. I suspect it had something to do with a male heir, somewhere or other, who, bored by such a peaceful existence, thought it might be more interesting if the question of authority were decided by brute force. But, alas, that theory will have to be taken up another time, for I am quickly wandering away from the original story I had intended to tell.

The empress about whom this story is written ruled over

her kingdom with wisdom and kindness as has already been indicated, and she was respected and admired by all who knew her. She had the utmost loyalty from her subjects, and all of the kingdoms that bordered hers were allies. Her husband and worthy assistant, the emperor, helped turn all of her inclinations into law, trusting her sense and reason without the slightest hesitation.

There was only one discernible eccentricity in the empress's character, and perhaps it was to be expected in one as worthy and remarkable as she. You see, this empress craved attention, and she was never happier than when she was in the spotlight, with all eyes upon her.

As the years passed, the empress's desire for attention grew, and she sometimes did things that would draw even more of it to her. Her dresses became bolder, made from cloth that was dyed in the brightest colors imaginable, and cut in such a way as to reveal the maximum amount of flesh. Too, she was apt to leave doors open where privacy was generally expected.

Her husband the emperor was well aware of this growing peculiarity in his wife's character, but as with everything else that pertained to her, he found it to be utterly charming and delightful.

Things went along quite happily for everyone in this way until the occurrence of one very singular event that took place during a great feast that had been arranged to celebrate the empress's birthday.

There was more than the usual amount of intrigue surrounding this birthday celebration, for it had been rumored that the empress had discovered a most exceptional new tailor whose designs had never before been seen in the region. The empress's clothing attracted interest even under ordinary circumstances, and so on this occasion, with the added mystery of the exciting new tailor, everyone's curiosity was especially piqued to see the empress's new clothes.

When the night of the great feast finally arrived, people were lined up early outside the castle, anxious for a glance at their beloved empress. The servants rushed to and fro in a flurry of excitement, speculating on what their mistress would be wearing. Even the emperor eagerly awaited his wife's grand entrance.

In due time the emperor and his guests gathered around the elegant dining table, while the servants stood alert at all points around the room, ready to jump at the slightest whim of any in the party.

Suddenly there was a hush throughout the room. The emperor looked up and beheld the empress.

She was as naked as the day she was born!

There were some sharp intakes of breath but, on the whole, everyone recovered quite admirably. A worldly duchess from a more populated city within the kingdom spoke up first.

"Your Highness," she said, with the most sincere inflection of respect, "you must give me the name of your new tailor. I have never before seen anything quite like it!"

Immediately the room became flooded with voices echoing the uniqueness and splendor of the empress's costume. Only the emperor remained silent, with a small smile of private amusement on his lips. He knew that the empress could do no wrong in the eyes of her subjects and that they would never dare to admit, even to themselves, that she wore no clothes. And yet he felt that she had gone too far. He realized that, as emperor, it was his duty to advise his wife on this matter. But how could he support her constantly growing need for attention, which was quickly becoming exhibitionism, without hindering her authority as ruler?

The emperor looked around the room and observed the unconditional adoration on the faces of the servants, as they graciously served their empress. His smile widened as an idea came to him. He remained quiet and thoughtful throughout the evening as he developed his plan. No one noticed the emperor's preoccupation for, as always, the empress commanded the lion's share of the attention.

A few weeks later the emperor smiled again as he dressed for the affair that he had so carefully planned. It had come together very nicely, indeed, and the empress had been more delighted than anyone by the idea. A theatrical production, right here in the castle! Why, it had been centuries since such things were done. She pleaded to know the details, but, of course, the emperor refused to tell her anything that might spoil the surprise. Even the servants, whom she supposed must be the performers in the feature, spoke not a word about it. Furthermore, the empress hadn't a clue about what talents they possessed, outside of their ordinary duties, and not once had she seen any of them practice!

Extensive renovations were made to convert one of the rooms in the castle into a magnificent theater. The room, which was located near the center of the castle, was chosen because it was completely round. All along the seamless walls, painters worked day and night to create exotic designs to awaken that portion of the brain that most appreciated those things theatrical. Theater seats were arranged on one side of the room, in rows that descended from the wall inward. But most peculiar was the theater box that was created for the empress and her husband, which was placed opposite the theater seats, and jutted out in all directions toward the small stage.

The little theater box was, in fact, a small room, constructed of panels that spanned out across the front. The panels were made from the finest crystal and were most exceptional, for each one offered a different viewpoint from which to see the event. So when looking through one panel, everything appeared precisely as it would through regular glass, but then, in looking through another, the same image would appear slightly more magnified and, in looking through yet another panel, there would be an even more magnified effect. Opera glasses were completely unnecessary, as, to see the event more closely, one would merely have to view it through a different panel.

For the final detail in these preparations, the emperor asked his wife to wear the same gown to the theater opening that she had worn to her birthday feast.

When the night of the big event finally came, the emperor walked into the castle theater a few moments after the empress arrived. He stopped for a moment when he saw her, standing alone in the little glass theater box. He wondered if she had any idea of what was to come. Would she enjoy the encounter that he had planned for her this evening? If he had read her correctly on the night of the great feast, and he felt certain that he had, she would indeed be intrigued by what he had so carefully arranged for her, no matter how frightening or unimaginable it might at first seem.

As he watched her through the glass, the emperor could clearly see every detail of his wife's body through the imaginary clothing she wore. She stood perfectly straight as she stared out through the crystal, looking this way and that, fascinated by the effect of the unusual panels.

The emperor casually joined the empress in the theater box. The servants, right on cue, were entering the theater and taking their places around the crystal room. The empress gasped when she saw her husband.

"How do you like my new clothes?" he asked, bowing slightly, as was his custom whenever he approached her.

Just as he expected, she covered her shock quickly and, raising her chin a little, she chided him lightly with, "So, you have discovered the identity of my new tailor!"

"Indeed I have," he replied, glancing nonchalantly through a crystal panel to see how the servants were faring, and mentally calculating how much longer before it was time for the show to begin. He pretended not to be aware of the fact that he was fully aroused. The empress, too, struggled to ignore his condition and maintain an outward appearance that was both dignified and aloof. But the accelerated rise and fall of her breasts gave evidence of an increased need for oxygen that only becomes necessary when accommodating a racing heart. The emperor noticed this and held back a smile. He had been hoping to achieve that response by the second part of Act One. This was going better than he had anticipated.

And it was time, indeed, to begin the presentation.

Very slowly, the emperor reached out his hand to touch the empress's breast. Shocked, the empress instinctively glanced out through the glass panels. At that moment, the lighting over her head seemed to get brighter, while the lights outside the theater box appeared to get dimmer. Even so, she could still see the servants clearly. They were looking expectantly at her and the emperor. She turned back to her husband questioningly, but he merely stared back at her, slowly moving his hand over her breasts, then down her belly and around the curve of her hips. A little shiver vibrated over her. One way or the other, the event had begun.

The emperor waited silently for the empress to comprehend the situation, thoroughly intrigued by the mixture of confusion and reluctant arousal that were evident in her expression.

"I thought there was to be a play, or...some...entertainment." Even as she said the words a slow dawning seemed to be creeping over her.

"There is," the emperor replied. He moved behind her then and, taking her shoulders in his hands, carefully turned her so that she was facing the crystal panels directly in front of the audience of eager faces. The empress stood frozen in place, looking at the faces of the men and women who were impatiently awaiting the entertainment that she was about to provide. In their expressions she saw a variety of reactions, ranging from intrigue, shock, amazement, excitement, amusement and even arousal. There were lascivious smiles on the faces of some of the younger male servants as they stared at her openly. She looked back in horror, even as a surge of excitement gushed through her loins.

The empress remained motionless, torn between a strong desire to stay and an anxiousness to leave. In that moment she was made aware of her darkest wish, and she feared it as vigorously as she wanted it. She responded to this dilemma much as a deer does, when its gaze is caught by a bright light in the dark night, and it becomes paralyzed with uncertainty.

The Emperor's lips were warm on the back of her neck as his hands moved deliberately downward, stroking her back and hips. Hypnotized, the empress silently watched the servants' eyes as they followed the motions of her husband's hands with rapt attention, especially as he brought them slowly around her waist and then upward, cupping her breasts. He caressed her with a knowing touch, brazenly fondling her. All the while he kept kissing her along her neck and back as she mutely stared at the audience's faces. Even when he suddenly and brutally squeezed the tips of her breasts, forcing a small gasp from her lips, she still did not take her eyes from those of the spectators, who stared, enthralled by the exhibition before them.

Frozen thus, the empress could only breathlessly anticipate the emperor's next move as his hands traveled slowly downward, ever so slowly, until at last they lightly grazed the tender flesh between her legs. Her audience's eyes followed his hands, as they circled round and round, just brushing her lightly, teasing her.

But the emperor was growing impatient to know if the empress was really willing to accept the part he had created for her in this drama and so, as the servants stared on, spellbound, he touched her more intimately, pushing his finger deep inside her, searching for her response to his unspoken question. He groaned with pleasure when he felt her soft, wet answer.

With the screen test so successfully concluded, the emperor could think of no reason to further delay the performance. He gently guided the empress's upper body forward so that she was bent at the waist. Instinctively, her hands reached out to lean on the crystal panel in front of her, in an attempt to gain leverage in her new position. Meanwhile the emperor spread her legs apart with his foot, keeping one hand on the small of her back to hold her in place.

"You are the scheduled performance, empress," he said, as he pushed himself into her.

The empress stood there, dazed, leaning weakly against the cool wall of glass, unable to think of anything but the roomful of servants who were silently watching while the emperor took her right before their eyes. She stared at the floor, still uncertain in the midst of the conflicting sensations that were flooding through her. But at length she felt herself being enticed out of her trance and succumbing to the exquisite pleasure building up within her. She slowly began to respond to her husband, self-consciously at first, with awkward little motions and thrusts, and meanwhile stifling her moans into tiny gasps and shrieks. But as the dreamlike quality of the event started to ebb away into the reality of what was happening, she became increasingly more excited, and her movements became more uninhibited and frantic, until at last she was pumping her hips against the emperor's in a frenzy of pleasure.

Though she kept her eyes glued to the floor, the empress was acutely aware that there were bystanders all around her, observing her every movement with keen interest. Even so, she slipped her hand between her legs to touch herself, shutting her own eyes tightly as she did so. That those staring eyes saw her hand and watched her please herself she doubted not and, as a matter of fact, this heightened her excitement. But still she could not bear to look at them directly. She was too self-conscious of the awkward movements and sounds she was making while thus engaged with the emperor in so intimate an act.

But what was the audience's response to the exhibition? she wondered. What were they thinking as they sat there, silently watching her and the emperor thrash about against each other with such wild abandon? She could feel the exquisite pleasure her husband was giving her, but what did it look like from their point of view?

These ruminations only increased her excitement, and suddenly she wanted more than anything to see the faces of the persons who had assembled around the glass room to watch. She turned her head sideways and tentatively looked up. Her whole body convulsed as she looked into the eyes of the multitude who silently stared at her in astonishment. Some were looking at the place where she and her husband were joined. Others watched her dangling breasts. Still others examined her face. Those gaping eyes watched in all different sizes, from normal to extra large, as they peered at her through the various panels for the desired effect. The empress shuddered as she tried to imagine the vision that presented itself from each vantage point. Wave after wave of pleasure seared through her, as she searched one face after the other, watching them watching her.

The empress's response increased her husband's excitement, and he became more aggressive, using her savagely as his passion continued to build. And throughout the event, those watchful eyes missed nothing. They caught all: from the crushing grip the emperor maintained on the empress's hips, to the small cries forced from her lips by his violent thrusts, to the poor lady's loss of footing under her husband's grueling pace. And even then, to the onlookers' amazement, the emperor did not relent; even when the empress's hands slipped from the wall onto the floor while she struggled frantically to right herself, he still continued mercilessly, seemingly unmindful of her plight. It was indeed shocking to see the empress in such a position, bent at the waist, with hands and feet grasping at the floor desperately while the emperor persisted in taking her so determinedly from behind.

But most remarkable of all was how the empress, throughout her extraordinary struggles and regardless of everything else, kept continually arching her neck in the direction of the servants, straining to keep sight of them, desperately scanning their faces, and frantically searching their eyes!

And in the midst of this, her entire body shuddered, time and again, exposing her pleasure in the performance.

Finally the emperor's excitement reached its peak, and the empress felt his warm wetness dripping down her legs. Even then, he still did not immediately release her, but remained inside her body, languid and self-possessed. A blush crept into her cheeks at the humiliating position she was obliged to maintain, for she had not been able to right herself since the loss of her balance, and still stood with her hands and feet on the floor, and her body bent awkwardly at the waist. Thus situated, all she could do was wait for the emperor's direction with a burning face, but even so, she still could not look away from the men and women who continued to stare at her. And in spite of her embarrassment, she could feel the tantalizing sensations building up inside of her all over again!

But at last the emperor waved the servants away. They, too, were reluctant to look away and, as they slowly walked out of the theater, they repeatedly turned their heads back for one last look.

Alone with his wife, the emperor at long last relieved her of her post and gently took her into his warm embrace. "You liked that, didn't you?" he asked, after watching her face for a moment. She assented with a shy blush, still too embarrassed to admit just how much she had liked it.

"I am glad, for you are scheduled to repeat the performance next week—this time for an audience of royals."

The empress pulled away from her husband and stared at him incredulously. She was still too overcome to speak, but it was beginning to dawn on her that, if what they had done ever got out, it would mean her certain ruin. It was, of course, reasonably possible that she could persuade the servants to keep quiet, but royals…?

The emperor knew her thoughts and laughed teasingly.

"Did I forget to tell you, my love? The crystal panels in our little theater box are magical. All who look into the theater box come under a spell which causes them to forget everything they see. Only those peering out through the panels from the inside maintain their memory." He gave her a big smile of self-satisfaction. "So you see, my dear, each and every time anyone comes to this theater, they will be as shocked and amazed and delighted by your performance as if it were the first time they were seeing it!"

"Do you mean to say that the servants will not remember what they just saw?" she cried. She could not contain her joy and began clapping her hands together excitedly.

"Do you like your new theater, empress?" her husband asked her, laughing.

"Oh, yes!" she replied happily.

Imagine, from now on she could have all the attention she could ever wish for (and then some), while never having to worry about the effect it would have on her position as ruler!

She thought of how exciting it had been to have all of those eyes upon her. What had they been thinking as they watched? She wondered what other things the emperor would do to her while servants and royals alike gazed on with interest.

The emperor laughed again as he watched the empress's expression change with her rushing thoughts.

"I have invited dukes and duchesses from all over our kingdom to attend our next production," he said. "Perhaps we should begin rehearsing for it now!"

And indeed they spent the rest of the evening doing just that.

The Goose Girl

There once lived a princess who had, since the day of her birth, been promised in marriage to a prince in a faraway kingdom. When the time at last came for the princess to go to her prince, there was great sorrow throughout her kingdom, for she was a kind and gentle princess who was loved by all. Her mother, the queen, was the most saddened by the event, and gathered for her daughter many rare treasures for her to take away with her.

Preparations took many months, and when they were completed there was such a procession of trunks that you could not see the beginning from the end. Stuffed within the massive trunks were assorted jewels of the rarest quality and brilliance, gold and silver accessories for the princess's every convenience, yards upon yards of the finest fabrics obtainable in every color of the rainbow, and too many other items to mention here—all of the very best quality and in great abundance. No small detail had been overlooked, so that there was included everything befitting a princess; indeed, many a queen would approve such a legacy.

These brimming trunks were carefully loaded onto long carts, which were then furnished with guards that had been selected from among the most devoted servants throughout the kingdom. In addition to this extravagant cargo, the princess was given, for her personal maid and companion, the beautiful daughter of the king's most trusted servant, a man who had himself descended from a long line of servants to the throne. This maid was a most agreeable selection to the princess, for she had been a cherished companion of hers since her childhood.

For her journey, the princess was given an enchanted horse that could speak, called Falada. Last of all, the princess was presented with a golden necklace from which hung a royal ring belonging to her betrothed prince. She was to return the ring to the prince upon their marriage.

When all was ready for departure, the entire castle turned out to wish the princess well and, at length, the journey was begun.

There was much excitement as the travelers set out, and the princess and her maid passed the first hours of their journey merrily. But soon they grew weary of the pace that was kept by the others, preferring to travel in a much more leisurely manner. In truth, the princess did not look forward to being married, and more particularly to marrying a prince whom she had never even met. That is not to say that she entertained hopes of somehow avoiding the marriage, for she was obedient and loyal, with that intractable conformity to duty that is characteristic of those with royal blood flowing through their veins. Still, it was her intention to enjoy her last moments of freedom for as long as possible.

Determined, therefore, not to be hurried into her inevitable destiny, she convinced her entourage to ride on ahead, allowing her and her maid to follow at their own pace. It was only a few days' ride on the princess's own royal lands, after all, and besides, no one in the procession was of the mind to deny the princess anything that she wished.

That first day of their journey was especially warm and, having taken many stops to rest, the princess and her companion soon fell far behind the rest of the group. Just as it was reaching late afternoon, the two came upon a clear stream and, delighting in the prospect of having a bath after such a long and tedious ride, agreed it was a perfect place to set up camp for the night.

Eagerly the ladies dismounted their horses, stripped off their dusty clothes and rushed headlong into the water. It felt wonderful to wash away the dust from the road.

But the princess was not used to attending to herself and in no time her hair was tangled in knots all around her. Seeing the princess's difficulty, her maid rushed to her side to lend assistance.

The luxuriously cool water caressed their weary limbs, and as the maid tenderly washed the princess's hair, the gentle rocking of the current brought their flesh repeatedly into contact. Before long, the subtle coercion of the waves had its effect, and the women were becoming increasingly enchanted by each other.

Once the princess's hair was washed and rinsed, she immediately set out to return the favor, so that the same process was repeated with the princess washing the hair of her maid. Meanwhile, both women became bolder, allowing their bodies to linger when the water brought them together, as if by accident, but really growing more and more aroused by the exquisite touch of the other's soft, womanly flesh. Their clean hair sparkled in the late afternoon sun.

But the princess was not yet willing to part with her charming maid and so, very leisurely, as if in a dream, she began to caress her, using the soap with her hands to give the appearance of washing the lady, but really only wanting to touch her more intimately. She was seized with a curiosity to know what the other woman felt like and how she compared with herself; but more than that she was aching with a need to please and be pleased by her.

It wasn't long before the maid was consumed by the same desires as the princess, and she too began to gently touch and explore her friend's body. They each marveled at the little peculiarities of their otherwise similar female charms.

Little by little they became more familiar with each other, discovering, as only women who indulge in this most extravagant form of self-love do, how exquisite it is to touch one so much like herself. Oh, how sweet to feel her lover's nipple harden between her fingers as she strokes the plump mound lovingly. How it excites her to glide her hand alongside the other's body and caress the enticing curves of waist and hip and round buttock. Her heart can hardly bear it when, searching below the small triangle of hair at the junction of two smooth legs, she finally discovers the tiny bud that causes the other to shudder—much in the same way that a touch there makes her shudder. She cannot resist slipping a finger into that womanly softness and feeling the warm, silky wetness within.

Covered in pearly suds, they eagerly caressed each other, discovering with delight that, despite their little distinctions, they were indeed very much alike.

With no more need to act under the ruse of bathing, the princess and her maid rinsed away the soap and waded to the shore. They leisurely dried each other's bodies, giggling, and teasing each other brazenly. They decided that one pallet was all they required for the night and excitedly set to work. Like two fairies in an enchanted wood they scurried about, delighting in their nakedness. The bedding was at last arranged, and timidly the maid lay down upon it.

The princess nestled alongside her maid and softly kissed her lips. The maid returned her kiss ardently, pressing her body against the princess's. They embraced like long-lost lovers, dropping one languorous kiss after another onto smooth, rosy lips. Between kisses they whispered endearments to each other, wholeheartedly declaring their affection, and it was exquisite for both when breasts touched breasts, legs glided over smooth legs, and shiny wet openings rubbed eagerly against the other. They were now terribly excited and longing for more.

The princess turned her body so that she was lying beside the maid, but facing the opposite direction. Both were new to the experience but each, as if by instinct, easily found her position before the other. With a quiver of anticipation, they first examined, then gently opened and tentatively licked the delicate flesh of the other. Soft moans escaped their lips as they discovered with delight the pleasure they could give each other in this way.

As their passion grew they clung more fervently to each other, and their hips undulated wildly against the tongues that worked at them with such eagerness. So fierce was their embrace that they appeared from a distance more like one creature than two, and their cries echoed through the forest while their horses silently looked on. All too soon it was over, but the princess and her maid continued to hold each other, trembling, and whispering sentiments of love to each other.

Later that night, the maid was awakened by a hard object that was lodged in the bedding beneath her. Feeling around in the tangled blankets she discovered the royal ring, which had fallen from the princess's neck during their lovemaking. She quickly snatched up the ring and hid it within her garments. A terrible plot, meanwhile, was slowly taking shape in her mind.

The maid knew that she should be pleased with her position as companion to the princess, for a kinder mistress could not be found in any kingdom. In fact, the princess treated her more like a sister than a servant. Perhaps it was this very benevolence of the princess's that caused the maid such discontent. Whatever the reason, the maid was intensely jealous of the princess, and coveted her many possessions and her lofty position. Most of all, she was envious that the princess was about to marry a prince. For the maid, marriage to a prince would once and for all give her the freedom and power she longed for. She would be a princess and have anything she desired.

Once the idea to betray her mistress had been conceived, it grew quickly, taking control of the maid's mind and forbidding all other thoughts to interfere. She ignored any feelings of sympathy for the princess, and even when it occurred to her that she may have to threaten the princess's life in order to realize her dream, she did not back down, though she shuddered at the thought. But she loved her own ambition far more than she loved the gentle princess. Still, she resolved to do all in her power not to harm the princess, as she once again went over the details of her plot in her mind, all the while clinging to the royal ring.

On the following day, the maid did not immediately reveal her intentions to the princess. Instead she brooded miserably throughout the morning as they resumed their travels.

About midday the pair passed by another stream. Quite thirsty, the princess said to her maid, "Please get down from your horse and fetch me some water."

But the maid refused, saying, "You may get it for yourself."

This shocked the princess, but she felt too kindly toward the girl to take the issue up with her as she should, and so, sliding down from her horse, she went to the stream to drink. But the princess's horse, Falada, marked all that occurred.

A little farther down the road the princess once again felt thirsty and, forgetting the earlier incident, she once more entreated her maid, saying, "Please get down from your horse and fetch me some water."

Again the maid refused the princess with a rude retort, and the princess was obliged to get the water for herself. But after drinking she stood up to find that her maid had dismounted also.

The look in her maid's eyes caused the princess's heart to grow cold with terror. It appeared as if the maid would kill her, but instead she ordered the princess to remove her royal robes and don her maid's clothing. This seemed an odd request, but the princess obeyed silently, even as she watched her maid put on her royal robes. Next, the maid mounted Falada, leaving her own nag for the princess to ride. The princess wondered at all that occurred, but said nothing, thinking it safer to wait until they reached the safety of the kingdom before questioning the maid's bizarre behavior. As for the maid, she kept postponing the moment when she would conclude her scheme, for she did not, in truth, take pleasure in the task ahead.

They traveled on for a time in this way, with the princess too frightened to speak and the maid solemnly pondering their fate. When at last they reached the fork in the road that marked the entrance of the betrothed prince's kingdom, the maid knew that she could delay no longer. She stopped the princess's horse and forced her to dismount.

Before the princess had time to speak the maid quickly produced a dagger. Pointing the dagger at the princess's heart, she gave her an ultimatum: to vow never to reveal her true identity to a single soul or else be killed. The princess was too shocked to speak, but the maid pressed the dagger forward, saying, "I know you will not break a royal vow, so vow now or die!"

What could the princess do? To save her own life she did as the maid demanded.

And so it happened just as the maid had planned, and when the two women arrived at their destination, the maid was immediately mistaken for the princess and received into the castle of the prince with much joy and celebration. As for the true princess, she was obliged to act as the maid. She was locked in her former maid's bedchamber, and forced to unpack her own possessions, which now belonged to the maid. The maid concluded this evil deed by sending out an order that all of the princess's entourage immediately be sent back to their former kingdom.

With her plan so very well carried out, the impostor princess lost no time in marrying the unsuspecting prince. But the true princess refused to serve her treacherous maid and, having no training or abilities for employment, could find no better position than tending to the royal geese in the courtyard. And that is how she came to be known as the "goose girl."

In this way, the prince and his bride lived happily together, but the goose girl, meanwhile, suffered a life of poverty and loneliness, where her only companions were the geese that she tended in the yard.

One day the prince wished to go out riding and, finding his own horse away to be shod, he mounted the princess's horse, Falada.

Away they rode at a fair gallop, for Falada was a fine horse, until they came to the fork in the road where the maid had forced the princess to make the fateful vow or lose her life. As they passed this place, Falada slowed down to a trot, and murmured, "This is where the servant girl would have killed your true princess if she did not vow to keep her true identity a secret."

The prince was shocked by this announcement, but he remained silent and allowed the horse to continue on in the same direction to see what else he could learn. They traveled on a bit farther and, at another place in the road, the horse once again slowed down, saying, "This is where the servant girl forced your true princess to exchange clothing with her."

Again the prince held his tongue and gently urged the horse onward. When they came to the large stream where the ladies had bathed, Falada came to a stop, saying, "This is where the servant girl and your true princess bathed and caressed each other, causing your royal ring to slip from the princess's neck and into the hands of her maid."

At this the prince abruptly turned Falada around and led her in a full gallop all the way back to his castle. Upon arriving there, he immediately sent for his wife, who he now perceived to be the maid. Though the penalty for such an act of treachery would usually have been severe, the prince had grown to deeply love his wife, servant or no. He did not wish to have her harmed, and he paced about thinking, trying to devise a proper punishment for her actions.

Suddenly he heard her footsteps behind him. She smiled at him innocently. "What is it you wish, husband?" she asked.

"I wish you to bring forth my true bride," he said quietly. At the unexpected request she turned deathly pale, but he touched her face gently, saying, "Do as I say."

Terrified of her fate, the lady rushed out to do his bidding. She quickly found the goose girl and told her of the prince's request. Upon seeing the terrified expression of her former maid, the true princess guessed that the prince had discovered their secret. To the amazement of her errant maid, the goose girl squeezed her hand and reassured her, saying, "I will not let harm come to you!" Though, in truth, she did not know how she would keep this promise. Indeed, there is no force on earth powerful enough to save a woman who does such harm to one of her own kind; and there is no force in heaven that will.

The maid was astonished by her former mistress's kindness. But alas! She could not undo what had already been done.

Trembling, and clinging to each other, the women approached the prince in his chamber. Seeing them so frightened, his heart was touched. But he had devised a retribution for his wife and was determined to see it through to the end.

"I wish to have what your deception has cheated me out of, wife," he stated. But looking at the goose girl, he nearly changed his mind, for her appearance was severely altered from the filth of the yard and the poor girl's lack of accommodations.

"But first she will have a bath," he decided. His wife started to ring for the servants, but he stopped her. "You will bathe her as you did in the stream," he instructed.

The prince's wife slowly undressed the goose girl. As she looked into the sympathetic eyes of the goose girl's dirty face she blushed with shame. She remembered suddenly how kind the princess had always been to her. She had regretted her treatment of the princess even before her secret had been discovered but, oh, how she had loved being a princess!

When the goose girl was completely undressed, the maid led her to an oversize tub filled with soapy water. The goose girl lowered herself into the water as the prince's wife bent over the tub to wash her.

"It will be easier if you bathe with her," interrupted her husband. "Is that not how you did it in the stream?"

Reluctantly, and with trembling fingers, his wife removed her own clothing and climbed into the tub. Despite her fears about her uncertain future, she could feel the familiar tingling welling up within her. Yet, in her present circumstance, it was as disturbing as it was pleasurable. Straddling the goose girl so that one knee was on either side of her hips, she began to carefully wash her snarled hair. Tears of regret ran down her lovely cheeks as she met the gentle eyes of the goose girl, who merely stared back at her former maid without a trace of anger. The prince watched silently as the goose girl boldly began to wash the hair of her former maid, just as she had in the stream on that night long ago.

Once their hair fell in clean, shining streaks around their slick bodies, the women took up the soap and slowly began to spread silky white suds over each other's bodies. The prince watched in amazement as the women bathed as intimately as they had done in the woods. Using only the soap and their hands, they washed each other thoroughly, leaving no part of the other untouched. The goose girl was so moved by the loveliness of her former maid that, forgetting the prince entirely, she brushed her lips across hers in a swift kiss. Oh, how she had agonized over what her maid had done to her while she was the goose girl! But mostly she was heartbroken, for she had meant every word of love that she had uttered that night in the woods.

Her former maid was tormented by too many conflicting feelings to respond to the kiss, and she abruptly stood up and stepped out of the tub.

The prince handed his wife a soft towel and instructed her to dry the body of the goose girl. She obeyed, and once again the goose girl returned the favor by doing the same for her.

Now the prince led the two women to his bed, saying in a matter-of-fact voice (though he was trembling in his absolute arousal), "Please, ladies, show me how you caressed each other beside the stream." The women hesitated, embarrassed. Their skin, which was flushed pink from their bath, tingled and burned with a mixture of self-consciousness and anticipation.

The prince, however, was impatient to know all that had passed between his wife and the princess. Their reluctance was like torture for him, and so he addressed the ladies who stood so enticingly before him impatiently, saying, "You have both betrayed me—one with her unfaithfulness and the other with her trickery. Under the law I may punish you however I wish. So you may both pay your debt to me, in full, here and now, or suffer the full penalty under the law." He spoke thus to the ladies, but only because he was in a highly agitated state and wished to spur them into action by whatever means necessary. In truth, the prince had completely forgiven both women when he beheld them together in the bath.

The women climbed awkwardly onto the bed and arranged themselves beside each other as they had before, with their heads facing in opposite directions at eye level with the other's hips. The prince watched silently as the women struggled to overcome their embarrassment. He didn't even blink, so loath was he to lose sight of them for even an instant as they tentatively touched each other's soft flesh, gently prying it open and exposing the inside completely to his gaze, and touching the tender, aching flesh with their tongues. He slowly paced up and down the length of the bed, first on one side and then on the other as he watched, desperately wanting to witness the apparition from every possible angle. He was mesmerized by the image of the goose girl's small, pink tongue as it worked its way into his wife's most private place, a place where he had thought himself to be the only trespasser. He was equally enthralled by the sight of his wife performing that same unorthodox ritual with her own sweet lips and tongue, so that he could not resist kissing her lips and tasting the evidence of what he was seeing there.

The goose girl did not even notice the prince, so happy was she to once again hold her maid in her arms. She caressed her brazenly with her lips and tongue, delighting in every shudder and quake of her lover's body in response to her touch.

And finally, the maid, who had experienced so many conflicting emotions that day, began to relax. It had all been so traumatic: beginning with the shame of having what she'd done exposed, followed by the terror of the consequences she might suffer for her actions, and finally, her stunned relief upon hearing her husband's declaration that her punishment would go no further than that room. She had been treated with more kindness than she deserved, and her punishment was, in fact, the very thing she had been dreaming of all these months, for, although she had fallen in love with her husband, she had not been able to completely forget her mistress's charms, or how exquisite their lovemaking had been.

It took her body a few minutes to recover from the shock of the day's upheaval, but finally, she began to lose herself in the princess's softness. Pretty soon the two were just as engrossed in each other as they had been that night by the stream.

Unable to endure being only a spectator for another moment, the prince gently pushed his wife away from her lover and knelt between the goose girl's legs. He stared into his wife's face.

"Touch her."

His wife reached down and touched the goose girl uncertainly with her fingers. The prince watched her fingers play along her opening, and he pressed against them gently, forcing her to be more intimate. He bent over to kiss his wife's lips as he did so. With his lips still touching hers, he whispered, "Tell me what she feels like."

She shuddered as a myriad of overpowering emotions clamored within her. Seemingly of their own accord, her lips whispered the true response to his question. "Soft, wet," and after a short pause, she added, "warm."

He pulled himself away from his wife so that he was once again facing the goose girl, but his eyes never left hers. The goose girl watched them both with interest, opening her legs wide and moaning lightly. He said to his wife, "Open her for me."

The maid felt a momentary pang of jealousy. But in the next instant she thought, *What right have I to be jealous, when I have taken all of this and more from the princess already? Furthermore, how can I feel jealous for one that which I love?* For she realized that she still loved the princess, and silently vowed that she would never betray her again.

Without further delay, the maid readied the goose girl for her husband's entry. She trembled under the influence of the many sensations mingling within her, and at length she was aware of her own throbbing need as she watched her husband slowly take the goose girl to mate. The goose girl moaned as she accepted from the prince the same pleasure he had given his wife so many times before. The prince watched his wife's face as she watched him, and it enhanced his pleasure.

The maid could not take her eyes from the image before her. When she saw the goose girl's flushed face she understood perfectly the pleasure she was feeling. And at last she was aware of how the goose girl had suffered because of her.

Without realizing her action, the maid reached out her hand and touched the goose girl's face, running her finger across her lips. Her hand slowly moved down, tracing the curve of her jaw and lower still, to caress a soft breast.

The goose girl moaned fretfully, caught up in the rapturous surge of her mounting pleasure. Suddenly the maid wanted to help her mistress if she could. She slowly moved her hand lower, and even lower still, until she reached the secret place she knew so well, where she worked her fingers gently, round and round, faster and faster.

The goose girl moaned louder, panting for air. The prince continued to thrust himself into her as he stared, fascinated, at his wife. She smiled as she continued to massage the little swollen mound, whirling it round and round, gently but firmly. She was getting closer.

The maid bent down to kiss her mistress' feverish lips. The goose girl whimpered and moaned. And still, the prince thrust himself into her. And his wife's fingers kept going round and round.

Suddenly the goose girl's eyes grew wide, and her body trembled violently as she cried out. In a rush of emotion she embraced her maid and kissed her repeatedly.

But there was still the matter of the prince. The maid looked up at her husband.

"Lie down, wife," he demanded.

She shivered with anticipation, even as she suddenly burst into tears.

The goose girl immediately rushed to her aid and held her close, but the prince gently pried his wife away from her.

He pulled his wife into his arms, where he took her, gently and lovingly, even as the goose girl looked on with interest. He kissed his wife's wet cheeks and attempted to soothe her, saying, "You are my rightful wife, for it is you who really wished to marry me." He knew that the goose girl would not have made him happy, and besides, it was too late, now that he had already fallen in love with her maid.

At hearing his declaration, his wife was filled with joy. She gazed at the goose girl, while her husband continued to gently make love to her. The goose girl snuggled closer to her and gently kissed her lips.

The maid slowly wound her arms around the goose girl, pulling her so close that their breasts were pressed tightly together. Thrilling sensations shot through her as she divided herself between her two lovers. From the waist up, she clung to the goose girl, who whispered little endearments between kisses, and pinched her nipples teasingly.

But from the waist down the maid was engaged in a much more tumultuous embrace with her husband, the prince. She clutched him with her legs as he thrust himself repeatedly into her, his eyes hungrily watching the two women clinging so fetchingly to each other. And once again, the goose girl returned a favor to her friend, by carefully reaching her hand down to the place where she and her husband were joined, and knowingly caressing her just above that opening. The maid clung desperately to both the goose girl and her husband as she screamed out her pleasure.

The prince now wanted his wife all to himself and, gently pushing aside the goose girl, he leaned forward to claim her lips with his, pushing her legs forward as he did so. This movement had the effect of spreading her body wider apart to better receive him, and he at last gave in to his own desire to be satisfied. The goose girl watched with interest as the prince satisfied himself with his wife.

And later, when the three lay quietly together, the former maid reached for the true princess, suddenly anxious to somehow make amends to her for all that she had suffered. She would never again harm another woman in an effort to benefit herself!

"You must come to the castle and live as a royal princess," she begged. "I shall be your maid and will work day and night to make everything up to you!"

Her husband lifted his head from the bed, about to protest her suggestion, but the goose girl interrupted him. "If you truly wish for me to live in this castle, I shall most happily agree, but I do not think it would be appropriate for a princess to act as my maid."

"But we all know I am not really a princess," uttered the repentant maid.

"But you are," argued the former goose girl.

"Indeed you are!" the prince spoke up. "I should hope, anyway, that marrying me would raise your status from that of a mere maid!" Both princesses laughed.

The prince rested again, while the princesses whispered endearments to each other and excitedly made plans for the future—their future, together. And again, it never occurred to either princess to consult the prince on any of these matters.

But, strange as it may seem, the prince did not mind. In fact, he has never been known to utter a single complaint about any of his wife's decisions since that day!

The Sheep in
Wolves' Clothing

I am a lady. I always conduct myself in a manner that is befitting a lady. And for my efforts I am duly rewarded, as are all ladies, with respect from the men and women who are my peers. This may seem small reward for the difficulties one faces in meeting the stringent expectations placed upon ladies, and admittedly, as the years slip past me, I do find myself more and more aware of the limitations that enclose me and the resulting deficiency of new opportunities presented me. But what are my alternatives?

This is not to say that I regret the decisions I have made. Of all the possible lifestyles I could have chosen as a woman, this was, without a doubt, the most tolerable one for me. It is just that I can't help wondering why it is only for women that the boundaries between the limited choices remain so distinct.

Have you ever noticed, for instance, how women with a strong maternal instinct tend to lose other aspects of their personalities upon having a child? Either from within herself or from without, I truly know not which, she appears to feel some kind of threat against her very right to be a mother, should she engage in any activity perceived as nonmaternal. She forgoes opportunities for professional advancement and denies her sexuality, dressing herself primly, sometimes even matching her own clothing to that of her children. Eventually opportunities that are sexual or professional diminish, and she becomes one dimensional and dull to anyone out of diapers.

Then, of course, there is the woman who chooses the professional lifestyle. Her peers are not as tolerant as those of the mother. She is in dangerous territory and cannot yield to the less sophisticated of her natural tendencies, lest she be deemed "unprofessional" and lose all that she has worked so hard for. She must be very careful how she presents herself and how she behaves. If she has children, she seems constantly weighed down by guilt, for to remain successful in her career it is necessary to overcome those maternal instincts that might be considered weak and unprofessional by her contemporaries.

Surely the worst fate by far, though, is that of the woman who chooses sexuality as her predominating course in life—usually a choice that is discovered on the path of least resistance, or is not even a choice at all, but an only option. Though this woman appears to be admired by men, she is really quite lonely, for they merely use her. She parades around in skimpy clothing, dangling the only carrot she believes to be in her possession, and her one and only chance for finding love and security. She allows herself to be exploited, only to invariably end up with nothing, for she alienates other women and relieves men of all accountability. She sometimes even loses her right to the maternal part of herself altogether, if she is naive enough to try and breach the boundaries of these two lifestyles and someone decides to call her on it.

Men, of course, have no such boundaries. And yet men seem to be the ones most determined to keep women's boundaries intact. I'm not sure why this is, since it most definitely makes things almost as unpleasant for them as for women. But it seems these boundaries produce a small measure of safety for men. They help define the women in their lives. It is not a foolproof plan, of course, but it works well enough and, I suppose, in their estimation, it is worth the cost.

As I have already stated, I have never regretted the choice I made, but rather that I had to make a choice to begin with. And though I am as happy as a woman within my boundaries can be, I have sometimes wondered what it would be like to temporarily escape into a different reality.

But how could I escape, even briefly, without risking everything?

I had given this much thought, especially in recent years, and had come to realize that there was only one answer. I would have to temporarily become someone else. But who?

This was a significant question for, if I were in fact going to conduct such an experiment, I would most assuredly want to gain the maximum amount of pleasure from the experience. For me, there was only one person who could help me realize my objective.

One evening, I approached my husband with the matter—not directly, of course; that would have indeed been foolish. I did not want to terrify or alienate him. But I needed his participation, even if unwittingly, as well as the benefit of his experience. The irony of the situation did not escape me, and I admit I was somewhat displeased by it, but this was not the time to resent that my husband, simply because he was a man, was entitled to have such experiences at his disposal while I was not.

I generally have very little difficulty getting what I want from my husband. He is kind and gentle, as far as husbands go, and over the years I have developed a fairly methodical approach to handling him. It is a rather roundabout way of getting something, I confess, and perhaps a bit childish too, but it works so well that I am hard-pressed to find a better method. I will divulge my strategy here, in case you have a mind to test it for yourself.

Always when I want something from my husband, I first question his love for me. This sets the tone I want, for it puts him in the position where he is making a declaration that in a few moments I will give him the opportunity to prove. With such an advantageous start, it seems unlikely indeed that one could fail. Besides that, I dearly love to hear him say it.

Next I make my husband aware that I want something from him, but I always ask if he will do it before I tell him what it is! He will generally answer in the affirmative, even if there is a tiny pause before he does so, and sometimes even a little disclaimer, such as, "if I can," or something to that effect. But I do not pay much attention to those. The important thing is that, like most husbands, he is willing to please me if he can. It is always more agreeable to my husband to please me when he imagines himself a wonderful benefactor by doing so. What does it matter if I sometimes think I should be entitled to these little "gifts," without having to appeal to my husband's ego? Such thoughts are not worth developing, for they are obstacles between a woman and what she wants. They are mere romantic notions that, if allowed, will interfere with the objectives of a lady. And furthermore, they have nothing whatever to do with love, for whatever his faults, I know that my husband loves me.

But in this particular instance, I was still uneasy about telling my husband what it was that I wanted. I knew that the thing would at first be distasteful to him, so I delayed a little longer, warning him that it would be difficult, but stressing its importance to me. So heartfelt was my supplication that I actually summoned tears to my eyes, and was even compelled to pause a moment in order to compose myself before I could continue. With the utmost concern, my husband took my hands in his and assured me fervently that he would indeed do everything in his power to fulfill my wish to the letter. Having his full commitment, I proceeded.

"My wish, dear husband, is to know the intimate details of the most unique and exciting sexual encounter you have experienced." I watched his concern turn to shock. Then he laughed. I suppose it was a silly thing for me to have made such a fuss about, but you must realize that, as a proper lady, very little was expected of me in the bedroom. Indeed, very little happened there at all, of late. I worried that he would not take me seriously.

Slowly his laughter died down, and he gave me a fatherly smile. Just as I had feared, he was about to placate me with one of our own dull experiences. I placed my hand on his lips.

"Before you answer my request, hear me out," I entreated. "I know you love me and I am convinced of your respect. Because of these two things (things that I deeply value), I believe I must be eliminated from the compilation of memories from which you will choose. I am not looking for a story of romance or love. I want only to hear of your most memorable, unusual and exciting sexual encounter with a woman—no matter how shocking, horrifying or embarrassing. All I ask is that you truly pick out the very best incident you can remember, and that you do not play it down to spare my feelings."

I thought I knew the meaning behind every expression that marked my husband's handsome features, but I had never before seen that particular look on his face. He opened his mouth to speak, and then closed it again.

I realized then that he did, in fact, have such a memory. It was in his mind at that very moment! My heart began to beat faster. I must know it! Real tears flooded my eyes this time as I grasped his hands urgently.

"I know it's an odd request, but I really want to know about it," I told him. Truly, the only other hope I had of gaining knowledge about such matters would have been for me to turn to a total stranger, and I was not quite that dissatisfied with my situation yet!

My husband ultimately gave in, of course, but I vow, it was more difficult than the time I wanted that terribly expensive diamond bracelet!

He was genuinely uncomfortable when he at last began to relate the incident to me. It was an experience that he had in his youth, many years ago. As he reluctantly described the affair to me, there was no doubt that my husband told the truth, for the expression on his face combined with the slight quaver in his voice thoroughly convinced me of the authenticity of all he said. And luckily, the incident did not repulse me. It was something I had never tried before, something I assumed my husband was not interested in, but then, it wasn't exactly something a man would be comfortable suggesting to a lady like me. How odd that the mere thought of it should send thrills of excitement through me! Yes, this had been a wise course to take. I now knew whose shoes I would borrow to escape my reality and sample the delights of a vastly different existence.

I asked my husband many questions. After a while, and especially once he saw that I was not hurt or disgusted, he became more comfortable. He answered all of my questions quite satisfactorily. He told me everything he knew about the woman, though it was limited since he had only seen her out that one time. How sad the boundaries can be for those women! I could almost have been jealous of her, except that, even after giving my husband such unforgettable pleasure, she had not managed to interest him in knowing her further.

My husband knew nothing of my reasons for my bizarre request, and I kept them intentionally from him. I wanted everything to be a wonderful surprise.

I prepared for days. And even when all was arranged to the minutest detail I repeatedly delayed, for I confess that I was exceedingly nervous.

And then, one day, I was ready. It happened quite accidentally really. Out of curiosity, I had slipped on the blond wig I had purchased for this occasion and glanced at myself in the mirror. My heart instantly began to race. I actually had butterflies fluttering wildly in my stomach! Yes, I was most certainly ready.

I slowly and carefully applied the new makeup I had purchased. First, I spread the dark, seductive charcoal color around my eyes, which made them look much larger than they are. Then came the lipstick. It had been at least ten years since I had worn lipstick, but I was certain that I had never worn that particular shade of red. I couldn't stop myself from giggling as I applied it to my lips. I felt a little like a child, dressing up in someone else's clothes.

Next there were the stockings. It is hard to believe that women had to contend with those before pantyhose came along. But what a delightful feeling when you wear them without panties! Being exposed to the air like that. Nice. Again I couldn't suppress a giggle. I hoped I wasn't going to make a fool of myself by laughing through the entire event.

A drink would have helped, but I was determined to wait until the last minute and then have only one. I did not want to get tipsy, after all. I wanted all my senses to be acutely aware so that I would feel every single sensation as it came over me.

Once I had put on the wig, makeup and stockings, I was finished. It felt like a part of me was missing, for I was never the sort that was comfortable without clothing, but there was no turning back now.

Having that much decided, I stood wide-eyed before the mirror. The woman that stared back at me looked strangely vulnerable. She was beautiful, with that poignant, forlorn beauty that belongs to those women who humbly present themselves on lace and silken platters, dressing up as best they can, in the hopes that this will bring them love, fame, money or happiness. And I thought to myself, *Why, any woman can do this. It's as easy as buying a costume!* My bright-red lips smiled back at me.

Suddenly I remembered one last thing. I fished through the makeup until I located a brown liner pencil. Then, very carefully, I drew a cute little mole right above my lip. There. Perfect! I allowed myself one more nervous giggle.

As usual, my husband came home right on time. I hid myself in the shadows of our dining room until I should decide the moment was right. My heart pounded ridiculously in my breast. Was it my very own, familiar husband I was hiding from? He came through the front door, as always, calling my name. But on this occasion I didn't answer him. I wanted every single detail of this evening to be different, memorable.

He called out my name a second time. I heard him ascend

the staircase, taking the steps two at a time. There was a shuffling sound upstairs as he called for me again, and then yet again. My heart was hammering painfully. I was almost afraid. It was a similar feeling to the one I had when playing hide and seek as a child.

I heard his footsteps on the stairs, this time descending. There was concern now present in his voice as he walked into the kitchen and again called out my name. Finally I stood up and slipped quietly into the living room. I stood inconspicuously alongside one wall in the large room.

In a few minutes he came into the living room and paused, scratching his head. I stood perfectly quiet and still as I watched him. After a moment he felt my presence. He turned his head precisely to where I stood frozen against the wall. Shock overtook his countenance. At first he did not even appear to recognize me.

I did not laugh, or even smile, for that matter. A new emotion was coming over me, stifling my earlier urges to giggle. I could hardly breathe while my husband stood gaping at me. But at last his confusion disassembled, and in both our eyes there was recognition. He knew me. And I knew him. He realized what I wanted him to do, and I, of course, had my script memorized.

He didn't say a word as he slowly walked toward me. His eyes traveled over me, missing nothing. A smile began to form upon his lips, but then just as quickly disappeared. As we stared into each other's eyes he was suddenly very serious.

"Are you sure you want to do this?" he asked softly.

This almost brought tears to my eyes, but I quickly blinked them back. His love and concern were what I lived for, but tonight I wanted something else from him. We would go back to that afterwards. I resisted the urge to rush into his arms and tell him how much I loved him.

Instead I jerked my chin up haughtily and assumed an indifferent tone. "That's up to you," I replied, holding his gaze, and adding slickly, "And depends on how much money you have." It did not sound like my voice that was speaking.

"I've got plenty of money," he countered, playing along coolly. "And I heard you're the woman who will give me what I want."

"Why don't you tell me what you want, and then I'll tell you if I can help you or not," I said evenly.

"You know what I want," he replied simply. "It's what every man wants when he comes to you. They say it's your specialty."

"Yes," I confessed, trembling slightly. "I think I do know what you want."

"Let's not waste any more time then," he said, removing his clothes.

I paused for a moment, watching him undress. I could see the evidence of his excitement in his pants. I could not remember the last time I saw that. As I stared at him, I struggled for every breath, my heart raced so. At last he stood naked before me. He was fully aroused.

"Where would you like me?" I asked him, getting right down to business. That's what this was supposed to be to me, after all.

He looked around our living room like he was seeing it for the first time. Finally he pointed to a small, square ottoman, the kind used for resting one's feet. "Bend over that."

I sauntered by him to comply with his direction. As I passed him I handed him a small tube of lubricant. "For what you want, you'll need this," I said, trying desperately to appear casual. I did not like to wander from the original script too much, but I knew I would need something to ease the discomfort I was sure to experience with my first time.

I bent over the ottoman in the wanton manner I imagined that other woman having done, based on the information my husband had provided. In truth, I had practiced the position a number of times when I was alone, trying out various places throughout our living room, and each time it had left me trembling and expectant to be sprawled out in such a manner. My husband, meanwhile, was preparing himself with the lubricant I had given him. I waited, reveling in the strange sensations that accompanied the full exposure my position presented of me. I wondered what that other woman had felt on that memorable night so long ago. As for me, I had never been so strangely excited before.

Suddenly I felt my husband near me. He pushed me forward slightly, maneuvering me, I knew, so that I was in the exact position that she had been in. When I was settled like he wanted, my head and forearms rested on the floor, and my knees rested on the ottoman, spread wide apart. In this position my hips were forced impossibly high into the air and opened very wide.

Terror and manic excitement made me light-headed, giving me a dreamlike impression of those first few moments. But when I felt his hands grasping my hips in readiness for what was coming, I suddenly became acutely aware of everything around me. It seemed that all my senses were heightened, so that every detail appeared magnified and distinct.

I held my breath as I felt my husband's hardness pressing against my nether opening. My hips instinctively contracted, wanting to close and move forward to escape him. But both my position and his grasp on my hips would allow no such escape, and so I was obliged to remain still as he forced himself into me. In spite of my good intentions, I cried out.

My husband immediately stopped. He did not withdraw, but he held himself perfectly still where he was. There were tears of disappointment in my eyes. I had not expected that first, stinging pain.

But in the very next moment the sting began to subside. Even so, it was still terribly uncomfortable. Notwithstanding the pain and discomfort, I was still amazingly aroused. And I was far from ready to give up on the experience.

I can't stop now, I thought. *I have come too far. Besides, if she could do it, I can too!*

With renewed determination, I arched my back, pushing my hips upward and opening myself further to my husband. He groaned when I did this, and his fingers dug into my flesh. He advanced very slowly, carefully urging himself into me, and I could tell from his groans that he was using every bit of restraint he possessed to go slowly. Even so, I had to bite my lip to avoid crying out again.

But at last he was fully inside me. The combination of shock, excitement, and discomfort was like nothing I had ever experienced before. As I became accustomed to the discomfort, I almost felt disappointment, so exquisite had that aspect of the intimacy been for me.

He withdrew gradually and then once again pushed himself forward slowly. He was being very careful and gentle because it was me. But I did not want to be me tonight. I wanted to be her. If I were really going to feel what she felt, all this tenderness would have to go.

"Do you like it?" I asked my husband, as he continued to move in and out of me slowly.

"Yes," he moaned.

"Do you like mine as much as you liked hers?" I pressed.

"Better!"

I was getting used to him now. It was still terribly difficult but, in an odd way, that added to the excitement. I began to move my hips, clenching and unclenching them as I remembered him describing her as having done. "Is this the way she moved?" I purred, as my hips awkwardly learned the rhythm.

"Yes!"

"She liked it hard and fast, didn't she?" I continued, remembering what he had told me.

"Yes, she liked it hard and fast," he repeated in a low voice that was barely perceptible.

"Give it to me like that, too," I ordered. "I want it hard and fast!"

"Honey," he groaned. "I don't want to hurt you." But he increased his pace.

"You didn't care if you hurt her," I argued. I worked my hips faster.

"She was different," he said, barely aware of what he was saying.

"Pretend that I am her," I goaded. And all at once I began to say the things that she had said to him, exactly as I remembered him telling me.

"Harder," I cried, pumping my hips furiously, massaging him within me. "Yes, that's better…now you're getting your money's worth…" I was beyond the point where I cared what I did or how I appeared. It was as if I really was that other woman, working as hard as I could to please a total stranger for money. And my husband was as lost as I was. He pounded himself into me with a violence I had never known he possessed. I shamelessly reached between my legs and caressed myself.

"What am I?" I asked him suddenly, needing to hear the words.

"What?" he was nearly oblivious of his surroundings.

"Tell me what I am," I pleaded.

"You're my wife…sweetheart…my adorable wife," he was quickly becoming incoherent.

"No!" I rubbed myself more vigorously. I couldn't stop myself. "Tell me I am what she was," I whispered.

He groaned.

"Now…please," I begged, still clenching and unclenching myself around him as he moved in and out of me. He was panting noisily. It occurred to me that, even with so little practice, I was already as good, or better, than she had been at this.

"Whore" he muttered. And with that he let out a thunderous yell, thrusting himself all the way in to the base. I felt him quivering inside me. "Oh, you're such a sweet little whore!"

I closed my eyes and shuddered as one pleasurable wave after another rippled through me. And in that split second I felt the utter abandon and exquisite pleasure of being a wanton whore, but without any of the remorse or loneliness that she would likely have felt afterward.

Later, my husband clung to me even in his sleep, while I— too exhilarated to rest—recalled the night's events in minute detail. If I had not felt the telltale tenderness in my backside, I would not have believed I had actually done it. And as for my husband, I had never seen him so thoroughly shocked. But that was not his only response, and afterward, when he had taken me in his arms, he was trembling as violently as I was.

A smile of triumph spread over my lips as I snuggled against my husband's warm body. His arms instinctively tightened around me. I had managed to step outside the boundaries that for so long defined my existence, and with very pleasant results. In fact, one could say it was a complete success. Not only had I discovered a new pleasure, but in the process, I had managed to collect for myself a great boon from my husband's past. For there was no doubt in my mind that this new memory my husband and I had just created together replaced forever, in his mind, that other memory of so long ago.

And really, hadn't it been incredibly easy? Indeed, those women have nothing on any of us! Why, any lady can do what she does. It is simply a matter of changing one's appearance, just as the proverbial wolf who dons the sheep's clothing or, I suppose in this case, you might say the sheep who dons the wolves' clothing!

I shall most definitely take on the alluring role again. But I must remember to tread carefully…lest I lose my way back!

The Ugly Duckling

Once upon a time there lived a husband and wife who had five daughters. The four older daughters were exceptionally beautiful, but the youngest daughter was thought by comparison to be gangly and awkward, with large bones and features that were less than perfect. Because of this, she was continually picked on by her sisters, and even her parents did little to conceal their disapproval of her, openly lamenting their ill luck in having such a child and wondering whether she would ever amount to anything. They all criticized the poor girl incessantly, saying such things as, "Perhaps if you ate less, you would be more petite," though she ate no more than any of the others, or, "If you rub lemons in your hair it would not be such a dull color." In truth, the unfortunate child went to bed hungry many a night and rubbed lemon after lemon into her hair, but nothing she did seemed to matter; there was always one thing or another that they would find wrong with her.

The townspeople were no different from her family; they insulted and criticized the youngest and plainest sister and other girls like her. Since her older sisters were thought to be so much more beautiful by comparison, the youngest sister soon came to be known to everyone as "the ugly duckling."

As the girls grew up, the four oldest daughters grew more and more beautiful. And as they grew more beautiful, they also grew more arrogant and insensitive. But the ugly duckling became more kind and generous with every day, so that, in spite of their constant mistreatment of her, each of her sisters preferred her company to any of the others'.

Soon the girls grew into women.

Now, the eldest of the five sisters was quite a striking woman, and thought to herself, "Why should I continue my education when I can earn a better living by simply letting men look upon my beauty?" For, indeed, in those days women could earn startling sums of money for displaying their beauty openly and explicitly to men who valued women according to that one quality. And so the eldest daughter went into the world with only that one asset to make her fortune.

The second-eldest sister was also very beautiful, and thought to herself, "Why should I have to do anything at all when men find me so attractive that they are quite willing to do everything for me?" And so she went out into the world with the viewpoint of making her fortune through the generosity of her many male admirers.

The third-eldest sister never had the opportunity to formulate a plan of any kind, for destiny intervened, and she was married to the young man whose child she found herself carrying.

The fourth sister thought, "Of what use are men to me when I am more beautiful than all three of my older sisters put together?" And she resolved to make a larger fortune than her other sisters without having to demean herself before men as they did. Having much confidence in her beauty, she set out to reach the highest achievement offered beautiful women of her time, which was to be a professional model of fashion and beauty.

Now the youngest sister, who was the ugly duckling, had no illusions about making her way in the world by means of her appearance, and so she perceived that she would be best served by continuing her education. She found a small university in the country, far away from the cruel prejudices of her hometown. Keeping to herself, she took a small cottage near the school campus and began her new life.

The ugly duckling immediately took to college life. She enjoyed her studies immensely and was strengthened by her growing knowledge of herself and the world around her. The people she chose to associate with did not seem to notice so very much that she was not beautiful, for they valued the many other qualities that she possessed. Without the constant reminders of her lack of perfect beauty, she slowly began to gain confidence in herself. She was repeatedly surprised by the continual flow of little joys in her life, and was happier than she had ever thought it possible for her to be.

One spring afternoon, as the ugly duckling rested languidly under the shade of a large tree in her yard, reading a book, there suddenly appeared a dark shadow directly above her. She looked up and beheld the most beautiful creature she had ever laid eyes upon.

He was well formed and dark, and stood smiling down at her. Half thinking the apparition to be a figment of her imagination (perhaps a character out of the romantic story she had been reading) she at first only stared mutely at him. Seeing her startled expression, the young man spoke to her in a friendly tone, explaining that he was merely passing through on his way to a nearby pond for an afternoon swim. Apparently the only way to reach the obscure little pond was by trespassing through the ugly duckling's yard!

The ugly duckling recognized the handsome young man as a fellow student in the same school that she attended. She secretly felt that she would enjoy seeing him on warm summer days as he made his way to the pond for an afternoon swim. Perhaps a bit too warmly, she informed him that he was perfectly welcome to cross her yard as often as he liked.

But the handsome young man did not immediately leave her upon gaining her consent, lingering instead to ask her about the book she was reading, her classes at the university, and other matters about herself that no man had ever asked her about before.

The ugly duckling's eyes shone with happiness as she chatted with her new friend, but suddenly the images of her sisters flashed before her and she remembered that she was ugly. At once she felt ashamed to have any man look upon her, and so, making up an excuse, she abruptly escaped into her cottage, where she watched from a small window as the young man left in the direction of the pond. He was energetic and healthy, with large arms and shoulders, and she wished for the thousandth time that she was beautiful like her sisters.

The days grew warmer and before long the trees and flowers were in full bloom. The young man now passed through the ugly duckling's yard nearly every day on his way to the pond beyond. And each time he passed he would stop and speak to her. Slowly she got over her self-consciousness around him, even looking forward to his visits, and they got to know each other better. Sometimes they would pass each other at the university, and he would thrill her by calling out to her.

One day the handsome young man asked the ugly duckling to join him at the pond. She abruptly declined, but from that day forward she felt a strange pull towards the pond, and often found herself wondering what the water was like, and how it would feel to splash around in it with her handsome friend.

And so it went, until one unusually warm summer morning, when the ugly duckling crept out of her bed very early and slipped down to the pond in her nightdress. She told herself she only wanted to look at the pond, but behold, it was more beautiful than she had imagined it. She glanced around guiltily. Certainly no one would be around at this hour of the morning. She would just slip into the cool water for a moment and then go back to her cottage. Before she could stop herself, her nightgown was shed and she was in the water.

The ugly duckling splashed the water all around her as she swam about happily. The water felt like silk on her skin. When she got tired of swimming she floated about, gazing up at the soft, hazy clouds that hovered in the blue summer sky. Occupied in this way, she completely forgot about the time.

The ugly duckling was not aware of his approach until she heard the huge splash as he jumped in the water. She stood perfectly still, frozen in horror as she waited for him to surface. She dearly hoped he didn't have his eyes open under the water, for she was ashamed to have him look at her body. And how on earth was she going to get out of the pond and put her nightgown back on?

Finally his head and arms bounced up to the surface. There was a huge smile on his beautiful face.

"I figured you for a natural girl, but I never dreamed you'd have the nerve," he said cheerfully.

So he had opened his eyes under the water! She was so horrified and embarrassed that tears came to her eyes. He was slowly swimming closer to her. She wanted to ask him to turn the other way so that she could get out of the water, but she was afraid of the sound she would make if she were to try and speak.

He was still smiling as he approached her. She saw that he was holding something out to her and, numbly reaching out her hand, she realized they were his swimming trunks. "Now we're even," he said, laughing.

She did not feel like she was in any respect "even" with the beautiful young man, however, and she merely stood there in awkward silence, holding his trunks in midair.

He seemed then, at last, to sense her discomfort. Very slowly he took the trunks from her stiff fingers and threw them over to the shore. He was standing very close to her, and she imagined that he was thinking about how ugly she was, and even expected that he would laugh at or insult her in the next moment, but to her utter shock he slowly lowered his head and gently placed his lips on hers.

The feeling was so glorious that she nearly lost her footing, but at the same moment, he took hold of her, drawing her even closer to him, so there was no danger of her going anywhere.

His body was exceedingly warm. His lips were demanding and insistent. His arms clutched her tighter, causing their bodies to press closer together. The water fluttered and swelled around them.

In the tumult of her first kiss, the ugly duckling forgot that she was ugly, and she returned his kiss with all the passion that she felt. She realized then that she was falling in love with him, and wondered if he guessed her feelings and, if so, what he felt. Just as she was dwelling on these thoughts, he drew his lips away from hers to search her eyes. He smiled at her uncertain expression, confessing that he loved her, too. Then he kissed her again, and again, and even then again! She clung to him, never wanting the kissing to stop.

But suddenly his kisses grew more passionate, and his hands were touching her everywhere. She discovered that she loved the feeling she got from pressing her naked body up against his. She felt dizzy with happiness to have his strong hands and beautiful lips upon her skin, but the kissing was becoming more and more urgent and demanding, and his body was rigidly pressing against hers. She was totally unprepared for what was happening. What's more, she could not help wondering if his declaration of love had a part in it.

With a little cry, she pulled herself away from him. She knew he cared for her in some way, but could he really love her? She would not allow herself to be taken for granted, ugly or not!

For good or for bad, I must know for certain what his intentions are respecting me, she thought, *and if I am agreeable to them, whatever they may be.*

For a moment they both stood apart, and for an instant he seemed almost angry at her. But at length, he smiled.

"I will turn and face the woods while you dress," he said kindly. "But will you wait for me?" he asked.

"Yes, I will wait for you," she promised.

"Well, if it isn't our own dear, plain little sister!" all four sisters exclaimed cheerfully.

The youngest of the five smiled warmly at her sisters. "I'm sorry I'm late," she said. "But how nice it is to see all of you again!"

"I must say," remarked the oldest sister to her younger sibling. "The years must have been good to you. I have truly never seen you looking better!"

The ugly duckling smiled. "I doubt the details of my life could keep your attention for a single moment, as exciting as I'm sure your own lives have been," she replied. She blushed slightly as she said this, though, for she was thinking of the previous night she had shared with her beloved husband and was certain that, even with all their beauty, her sisters could not have experienced greater happiness than her own.

"Exciting!" repeated the third eldest sister with bitterness. "I was cheated out of the excitement I should have had."

"At least *you* got married," snarled the second-eldest, even more bitterly.

"Married!" she returned. "Imprisoned would be a better word."

"Aren't you happy to be married?" asked the ugly duckling, shocked.

"Do I look happy to you?" she answered, with tears welling up in her beautiful eyes.

Her four sisters stared at her in surprise.

"Oh, my husband never loved me," she confessed. "When we were young, he was attracted to me, but he only wanted one thing. I mistook that for affection. I never stopped or held back to see what he really felt for me. I was so happy to have the attention and so sure that my beauty would make him love me. Then I got pregnant…and he was obliged to marry me. But he doesn't love me! Women are just replaceable objects to him. He has affairs while I stay home and take care of our children."

"My God," uttered the eldest. "And I thought I had it bad."

"I would give anything to have your life!" the unhappy lady pronounced.

"No, I don't think you would," the eldest sister rejoined. Then she turned to her sisters with her own sad tale.

"You see, I thought to make my fortune by showing my beauty openly to men, so I became an exotic entertainer. I figured I could earn a better living that way than through anything an education could teach me. And I was right about that at first. But you can only do this for a little while. Soon there are younger girls that come to take your place and you don't earn very much after that."

"Perhaps," said the unhappily married lady, without seeing the irony, "you should have married one of your admirers while you were still young."

"Then I would be in the same boat as you!" the eldest replied with disgust. "Besides, most of them were already married." She sighed unhappily before she went on. "Anyway, how could I ever trust a man after I had seen firsthand how lecherous their behavior becomes when they are not in their wives' sights?"

"It's quite true," said the second-eldest sister, who had made her way in life by selling even more of herself to men than her older sister. "Once you see that side of men you can never trust them." She looked sadly at her older sister and added, "And once you sell that part of yourself it's no longer your own. It becomes a tedious occupation. I have never genuinely enjoyed being with a man because it has never really been for me, or on my terms."

"You've made it so easy for men to treat you like that," said their unhappily married sister harshly, adding under her breath, "and the rest of us, too."

"Oh, so it's our fault that men are the way they are," her older sister replied defensively. "Why are women always so quick to blame the other women?"

"Maybe it's because you are willing to do for a fee things that men would otherwise have to prove themselves worthy of," she said resentfully, now worked up into full anger. "Lots of women, just like me, continually work to improve themselves—and they are, in fact, far more than their men deserve. But the men don't have to put forth any effort; yet they can have the most beautiful women imaginable at their fingertips if they have money."

"Well, it should make you happy to know that we have paid a high price in offering that service to men," her sister argued back.

"Yes, I see that you have," said her sister slowly. "But you *chose* the price you have paid in exchange for the fees you have collected. The rest of us have not made any such choice or collected any such fees, yet we have to pay the price right along with you!"

There was silence for a moment after this outburst.

The third-eldest sister sat brooding about her unhappy marriage while her older sister made an attempt to turn the subject around.

"You know," she said with a sigh, "it is true about the men. Most of my customers are fat, bald and ugly."

"Indeed," chipped in the fourth-eldest sister, who had remained silent up until this point. "It is because we are expected to be perfect, in a world where perfection doesn't exist. The standard is so high that no woman could possibly reach it. Meanwhile, the men just sit back and enjoy the show. They don't have to worry over their appearance because nobody ever seems to notice them. They are invisible."

The sisters laughed in agreement when they heard this.

"But you have reached physical perfection," interjected the ugly duckling, who had listened in silent shock to her sisters' confusing harangue. "I saw your picture on the cover of that prestigious magazine."

"I am ashamed of that picture," said her sister with emotion, gaining the full attention of her sisters, and then continuing with her own story as follows.

"I know I am a beautiful woman. I have dedicated my entire life to beauty! But that is not enough to satisfy the editors of the women's, ha, *women's*—" she paused over the word for emphasis before continuing "—magazines. How women can bear to read them is beyond me.

"Anyway, I found that I was not—indeed none of us were—good enough to grace the pages of those militant catalogs of female delusion and torture. Before I could even be accepted as a candidate I discovered that I would have to submit to a number of surgical alterations and virtually stop eating. All of this I did, and at last I was chosen for the magazine of which you spoke. But would you believe, even after all I had suffered and endured, in the end I was still not beautiful enough, and the picture was altered in the final draft." There were tears in her eyes as she looked at her youngest sister. "That picture is not one of me, but of a specter—the very same specter that is being held up before women to keep them racing after perfection." She looked around sadly at her sisters, and added, "It is the same specter that has ruined the lives of each and every one of us."

For some reason this brought their youngest sister to their attention. Almost simultaneously the women turned to her.

"What has life been like for you?" asked her oldest sister.

"Well, I am certainly satisfied with it," she answered humbly, not wishing in the least to gloat over her own happiness in light of what she had just heard.

"You continued your education, didn't you?" another sister asked. "What was it you studied?"

Timidly she began to tell her sisters about her studies, never at a loss for words when she spoke of the things she had learned. Yet their silence intimidated her, and her voice trailed off. No doubt they would think her life ridiculous.

But her older sisters did not mock her or laugh. They questioned her with interest and, at length, she told them about her many interests and her marriage and her little daughter. Feeling guilty over her own good fortune and happiness, she refrained from telling them about the many little joys in her life; like how her husband worked so hard to keep himself in tiptop shape for her, or how he never lost interest in making love to her. The sisters were too astute not to see these things in her face, however, and could not help feeling envy for the accomplishments of their youngest sibling, despite her supposed physical defects.

The third-eldest sister, being the bitterest of the four, could not help remarking, "It seems as if we would all have been better off to have been born ugly!"

The eldest sister immediately jumped to her youngest sister's defense, saying, "You're just jealous."

The youngest sister took courage by this. "I don't think it is because I am ugly that I am so happy," she said slowly, thinking. "Of course, I did not rely on good looks to do me any favors, and that was part of it. But mostly I felt that whatever I should seek out of life, I should first identify it for what it truly is, and then find out what it would cost me. And that is what I have done."

She looked at her sister who was so unhappily married and went on, "You said yourself that if you had held back and waited, you might have discovered that your husband did not really love you. But you allowed yourself to be flattered by his attentions, not realizing that they weren't really all that flattering because he didn't care very much for you at all."

She turned to her other sisters and continued, "Each of you

suffered similarly because you let yourselves be used for the moment as beautiful objects. You did get paid, but not enough considering that you traded your own requirements for a happy life for that payment. You've in a sense made men unaccountable for their actions."

After that, there seemed little left to say.

Finally inside the door to her house, her haven, the ugly duckling sighed in relief. It was late, but a welcoming light had been left on in the entranceway. There were newly cut flowers in a vase sitting on a small table. She took a moment to smell them, savoring everything about being home.

She continued on up the stairway until she came to a small bedroom at the top. She stepped inside, carefully making her way in the darkness to the small bed where the barely audible sleeping sounds drifted upward from a clutter of soft blankets. She stooped to kiss the tiny cheek, soft and warm. She adjusted the blankets as she admired her daughter, so beautiful like her aunts. She would teach her to enjoy her beauty but not to rely upon it.

She left her sleeping daughter and quietly made her way down the hall to the larger bedroom. Upon entering, she stopped for a moment and closed her eyes, breathing in deeply the familiar scents of his cologne as it mingled with her perfume. It was a warm night, and it delighted her to see the long, filmy curtains swaying gently with the breeze.

She removed her clothes and eased her way into the warm bed. He was awake, and without a word, took her in his arms and pulled her into his warmth. She nestled against him and felt the familiar hardening of his body.

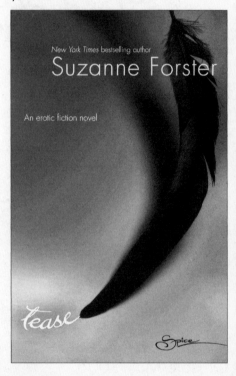

SPICE & BootyParlor.com

live your fantasy CONTEST

For the launch of our Spice line of books, we've teamed up with our friends at BootyParlor.com™ to offer you a chance to win an irresistibly sexy contest. Why not enter today?

Live Your Fantasy Romantic Island Getaway Contest

You could win a trip for two to the beautiful Jalousie Plantation Hotel™ on the gorgeous island of St. Lucia! Nothing is sexier than spending a full week at this tropical all-inclusive resort. All accommodations, airfares and meals are included! Even spa treatments— nothing's more sensuous.

Simply tell us about your most romantic fantasy—in 100 words or less— and you could win!